Dark, Witch & Creamy

Bewitched by Chocolate Mysteries

Book One

H.Y. Hanna

DEDICATION

To my husband, who is a wizard
with wit and words.

CONTENTS

CHAPTER ONE...1
CHAPTER TWO..14
CHAPTER THREE...25
CHAPTER FOUR..36
CHAPTER FIVE 47
CHAPTER SIX..58
CHAPTER SEVEN...73
CHAPTER EIGHT...80
CHAPTER NINE 92
CHAPTER TEN 98
CHAPTER ELEVEN..110
CHAPTER TWELVE 120
CHAPTER THIRTEEN 130
CHAPTER FOURTEEN 138
CHAPTER FIFTEEN 149
CHAPTER SIXTEEN...162
CHAPTER SEVENTEEN 168
CHAPTER EIGHTEEN.......................................177
CHAPTER NINETEEN 185
CHAPTER TWENTY..195
CHAPTER TWENTY-ONE 206
CHAPTER TWENTY-TWO...................................216
CHAPTER TWENTY-THREE 224
CHAPTER TWENTY-FOUR 235
CHAPTER TWENTY-FIVE...................................247
CHAPTER TWENTY-SIX.....................................255
CHAPTER TWENTY-SEVEN 264
ABOUT THE AUTHOR.......................................278

CHAPTER ONE

"I can't believe you're really gonna do this."

Caitlyn Le Fey looked up from the map she was holding and smiled at the pretty blonde girl who was frowning at her from across the table. Around them, the tearoom buzzed with the hum of conversation and the clink of china, while the gorgeous smell of fresh baking wafted from the kitchen.

"What do you mean?" she asked lightly as she helped herself to the last mouthful of scone from the plate in front of her. She savoured the rich, buttery bread slathered with home-made strawberry jam and clotted cream. *Mmm... they said the scones at the Little Stables Tearoom were the best in Oxfordshire and they were right.*

Caitlyn licked her fingers clean and smiled. "I'm just going for a drive in the Cotswolds."

"Not just *any* drive," the other girl protested. "You're driving out to a village where someone's been murdered by witchcraft!"

Caitlyn stifled the urge to roll her eyes. She loved her cousin, but sometimes Pomona's wild imagination could get a bit ridiculous. "That man wasn't murdered by witchcraft."

"Yes, he was! The papers are full of it!" Pomona picked up a tabloid newspaper from the table and waved it dramatically. "They said he was found by a stone circle!"

"So?"

"An ancient stone circle, Caitlyn! They're, like, the kind of place where pagan rituals and sacrifices take place. They said he was icy cold to the touch and they couldn't find a mark on him—"

"Anyone's body would feel cold if they'd been outdoors all night," said Caitlyn reasonably. "He probably had a heart attack."

"But he'd been fine earlier that evening! Half the village saw him at the local pub. And no one saw him go into the forest. He was a big man—he wouldn't have been easy to carry—so how did his body even get there?" Pomona leaned forwards and lowered her voice. "Maybe someone transported him there..."

Caitlyn grinned. "You mean, flew him on a broom?"

Pomona made a face and threw her napkin at her. "Ha. Ha. Very funny. Seriously, Tillyhenge could be a dangerous place. Are you sure you should go there?"

Caitlyn reached out a placating hand. "Hey... Pomie... It's just a sleepy little Cotswold village like any other, except that this one has a stone circle nearby—"

"That's exactly it!" said Pomona, her voice rising. "Don't you know that stone circles are sites of great magic? They're places on earth where the powers of nature come together—they're connected by ley lines."

"Ley lines?"

Pomona nodded earnestly. "Ancient invisible lines of energy. Stone circles are often where the ley lines meet. They're also places where druids and witches worship and perform their spells and stuff, 'cos the circles mark the points where you can open a doorway to the Otherworld—"

"Aww, come on," said Caitlyn, rolling her eyes. "I know you're really into all this occult stuff—but seriously, Pomie? Witches and druids? Doorways to the Otherworld? We're in twenty-first-century England, for heaven's sake!"

"There's still magic all around us... You just don't wanna see it," said Pomona, jutting out her bottom lip.

Caitlyn gave her an exasperated look. When it came to the paranormal, Pomona had a one-track mind. She was obsessed with witchcraft and magic, pagan rituals and the occult. Maybe it was the result of growing up in Hollywood or maybe it was just growing up with actress Mariah Sinclair for a mother.

That lady was almost as famous for her outlandish beliefs as for her glamorous looks. It was no wonder that Pomona still believed mermaids and unicorns were real!

As for herself, Caitlyn was grateful that she'd never lived in Beverly Hills much. Her mother, Barbara Le Fey, and Mariah had been sisters, but although Barbara had been in showbiz as well, the singer had preferred life away from the Hollywood parties and celebrity circuit. Barbara had been a free spirit and a hippy nomad, happiest when she was spending most of her life on the road. Even when she hadn't been touring and giving concerts, Barbara would choose unusual places to settle for several months, sometimes years—from a jungle villa in Bali to a converted church in the south of France, from a luxury caravan in the Australian Outback to a yacht in Tahiti...

As a child, Caitlyn had sometimes felt like a gypsy, always moving homes, barely staying anywhere long enough to make friends. It also meant that she didn't know what country to call her own. Barbara might be American but Caitlyn didn't feel like she belonged anywhere. In fact, the one place she had always been drawn to was England, although she couldn't explain why. Well, now that she knew the truth about herself, perhaps that made sense...

"Hello? Earth to Caitlyn?"

She blinked and refocused on her cousin. "Sorry, what were you saying?"

"I was saying that it's not just me. There are rumours going around here too. The locals agree that Tillyhenge has a reputation for being weird."

"Weird? What do you mean, weird?"

"Like... the weather is always different there. It could be sunny everywhere else but when you get there, it's grey and misty—or it's raining all over the Cotswolds but completely dry in Tillyhenge... And if you're driving, the GPS can't find it, no matter how you give the directions. In fact, it doesn't even show up on satellite images—they told me it's just a green blur, as if there's nothing there but forest!" Pomona shuddered. "Don't you think that's creepy?"

Caitlyn sighed impatiently. "That could just be coincidence. Even back in the States, you'd sometimes get rain in one part of town and not another—there's nothing weird or spooky about that. Anyway, who told you all these rumours?"

Pomona jerked her head in the direction of four little old ladies who were huddled around a table nearby. "Them. I started talking to them when you went to the restroom earlier. There's this bossy old hen called Mabel—she told me they know everything that goes on in the area. They're like the Gossip Mafia."

Caitlyn gave her a wry look. "Yeah, I know those old biddies. I've run into them a few times while staying in Oxford." She leaned towards Pomona and lowered her voice. "I think you've got to take anything they say with a big pinch of salt. They're known for having... uh... pretty vivid imaginations."

"Still... Caitlyn, you gotta listen to me. I have a bad feeling about this. And you know I'm slightly psychic, right?"

Caitlyn hid a smile.

"It's true!" said Pomona. "I have feelings about things. Remember that time when you fell off the yacht and I got my mom to call Aunt Barbara 'cos I knew something bad had happened to you? And the time I warned you about that scary skin rash?"

"You said I had Rocky Mountain spotted fever! It was actually chicken pox."

Pomona waved a dismissive hand. "Yeah, well, that's almost the same thing. Anyway, I'm telling you, I have a feeling about this." She reached out suddenly and grabbed Caitlyn's teacup. "Okay, look—I'm gonna read your tea leaves."

"Pomie..." Caitlyn groaned but her cousin ignored her, peering into the teacup and turning it this way and that.

"Hmm... ooh! Ooh! I see something!"

"What?" asked Caitlyn, curious in spite of herself.

Pomona smiled. "A tall, dark, handsome stranger is coming into your life."

Caitlyn groaned even louder. "Oh, give me a break—"

"Wait! There's more!"

Caitlyn gave her a wry look. "What? I'm going to receive a letter? Come into a lot of money?"

"No..." Pomona frowned. She turned the teacup.

"It looks like... it looks like a bar of chocolate."

"Chocolate?" Caitlyn said incredulously. "What, there's chocolate in my future? Or are you telling me that I'm going to put on weight?" She grinned. "Because I have to say, that's probably true, but I don't need some fortune-telling tea leaves to tell me that." She looked ruefully at the empty plate in front of her, then down at herself. "All this British baking is absolutely delicious but good grief, it's a killer on my hips."

Pomona gave her a scornful look. "Huh! You can't talk about hips until you've got hips like mine."

"Yeah, but you *own* your hips," said Caitlyn, looking enviously at her cousin's full figure. Pomona had a backside that deserved the name "booty" and she flaunted it with pride. Caitlyn wished that she had her cousin's confidence. Her own figure was what the English politely termed "pear-shaped"—she wasn't fat, exactly, but no matter how she tried, she couldn't seem to shift the weight off her hips and thighs.

"Your hips aren't the problem," said Pomona, eying her critically. "It's everything else. Look at the jeans you're wearing – they must be, like, ten years old!"

"They're comfortable," said Caitlyn defensively.

"Honey, you can be 'comfortable' when you're eighty! When you're twenty-two, you wanna be '*gorgeous*'. And you could be, if you just made a little effort! I mean, look at your hair—you've got the kind of red hair that other women can only get out of a bottle and green eyes like—"

"They're not green, they're hazel," said Caitlyn quickly. "And most of the time, they just look light brown."

Pomona gripped her hand eagerly. "Give me twenty minutes and some mascara and eye shadow, and I'll give you the most amazing green eyes you've ever seen. C'mon, Caitlyn, lemme do a makeover and—"

"No."

She pouted. "Aww... you're always saying no!"

"I'm not you, Pomie," said Caitlyn, giving her cousin a look of mingled admiration and resignation. "I'm no good with things like make-up and fashion. Even if you made me look amazing, I could never keep it up by myself."

"You could learn! Applying mascara isn't rocket science!" Pomona huffed in frustration. "You know what your problem is, Caitlyn? You're *afraid* of people looking at you. You're afraid of getting attention. But you can't go through life always skulking in the shadows."

Caitlyn sighed. She knew her cousin could never understand. Pomona loved being the centre of attention and revelled in the limelight. She could never relate to Caitlyn's desire to stay in the background.

"Well, I'm coming out of the shadows now, aren't I?" Caitlyn said lightly with a smile. "This little adventure to Tillyhenge—"

"That's different," said Pomona, frowning. She leaned forwards, suddenly serious. "I can feel it, in *here*." She pressed her ample bosom. "If you go to Tillyhenge today, you'll change the path of your life forever. Things will never be able to go back to what they used to be."

"Whoa..." Caitlyn leaned back at her cousin's ominous tone. "Honestly, Pomie, I think you're over-reacting. I'm just going for a drive and maybe staying a couple of days in a village in the Cotswolds. It's no big deal. Tourists do it every single day."

"Well, then go where they go," said Pomona. "Go to one of the other Cotswold villages where tourists usually visit. Like Burford or Lower Slaughter—or why don't you stay a couple of days here in Meadowford-on-Smythe? It's gorgeous. Why d'you have to go to Tillyhenge?"

"Because that's where I'll find answers."

Caitlyn raised her right hand unconsciously to touch the runestone attached to the ribbon around her neck. Her fingers slid over the stone, tracing the symbols carved onto the smooth surface, even though she knew the shapes by heart already. She had traced them a million times, ever since she was a little girl, although she still didn't know what they meant. It was one of the many mysteries from her past, one of the things she needed answers to.

Pomona dropped her gaze to the stone. "Are you sure the letter didn't say anything else about that?"

Caitlyn shook her head, thinking about the letter that had turned her life upside-down. She had barely recovered from the news of Barbara Le Fey's death in a car accident before she had been called into a private meeting with the singer's lawyers. And there, she had been handed a sealed letter—a letter Barbara had instructed to be given only upon her death—and Caitlyn had opened it to discover that the woman she had called "Mom" all her life wasn't her mother at all.

To be honest, she had never felt very close to Barbara—something which had always vaguely bothered her, although it was hardly surprising since she had been almost completely brought up by her British nanny. Barbara Le Fey had adopted a child on a whim and had soon lost interest when the novelty had worn off. Oh, she had always been generous and kind, and Caitlyn had never wanted for anything, but Barbara had remained a distant figure in Caitlyn's life. Still, it had been a shock to discover that Barbara wasn't her "real mother".

"I've read the letter so many times, I practically know it by heart," said Caitlyn. "It didn't mention the runestone, other than to say that it had been around my neck when I was found as a baby by the side of the road—"

"I still can't get over that," said Pomona, laughing. "Seriously, it sounds like something out of a fairytale! When you first told me about it, I thought Aunt Barbara must have been joking."

"So did I," Caitlyn admitted. "I wasn't sure what to believe. But then after the funeral, I got talking to Jim Stanton, Barbara's agent. He'd been with Barbara for years and he told me that he'd been in the car the day she found me. It happened exactly like the letter described. They were on their way to some country house party and they'd taken a detour down a country lane... and then they saw this tiny baby, wrapped up in blankets, propped against a bush at the side of the road..."

"Jeez, you must have only been, like, a few hours old," said Pomona.

"Exactly!" said Caitlyn. "That's what Barbara said the doctors thought when they examined me—which means I must have been born around here!"

"Okay, but I still don't get how that's connected to Tillyhenge. Why d'you think you'll get answers there?"

Caitlyn leaned forwards earnestly to explain. "I got talking to a professor at Oxford University a few days ago and he told me that researchers have discovered 'hidden engravings' on the surface of the giant stones at Stonehenge."

"So?"

"So... he said the symbols on my runestone reminded him of those engravings. Don't you think that's just too much of a coincidence?" she asked impatiently, as she saw Pomona's blank stare. "Look, my runestone is engraved with these symbols, which are similar to those carved on Stonehenge, a famous stone circle... but there is a local stone circle near a village called Tillyhenge and I was found in the same area. There has to be a connection and the only way to find some answers is to go to Tillyhenge myself."

Pomona heaved a sigh. "All right. I can see that I'm not gonna change your mind." She gripped Caitlyn's hand tightly. "But promise me you'll be careful? I don't want anything to happen to you. You're... you're like my sister. The only sister I have."

Caitlyn felt a rush of affection for the other girl. Whatever else happened, she knew she would always have Pomona as family. They might not have grown up in the same city together and Pomona's glamorous Hollywood lifestyle was very different to the hippy, nomadic life that Caitlyn had led, but somehow they'd instantly bonded from the first time they'd met. Caitlyn had always looked forward eagerly to the school vacations and holidays when Pomona would join them for a while on the road.

She squeezed her cousin's hand. "I promise I'll be careful." Then she glanced at her watch. "You'd better get going otherwise you'll miss the train back to London. Don't forget, you've got to go back to Oxford first to catch it."

"You sure you don't want me to come with you?" asked Pomona, rising slowly.

Caitlyn hesitated. A part of her desperately wanted her cousin to go with her. She was nervous about what she would find and she didn't want to face it alone. But she also wanted to keep a low profile, and—with her glamorous looks and flamboyant dress sense—Pomona drew attention wherever she went. Her cousin had already been getting stares the whole time they were in this tearoom.

"No, I'll be fine," said Caitlyn, pinning a bright smile on her face.

"Call me tonight and let me know what's happening," said Pomona over her shoulder as she headed towards the door. "And make sure you don't meet any black cats!"

Caitlyn sat for a long moment after her cousin had gone, feeling suddenly very alone. She almost picked up her phone to call Pomona and say she'd changed her mind, to ask her cousin to go to Tillyhenge with her.

Then she took a deep breath, drained her teacup, and stood up. No, this was something she had to do herself. In a strange way, she felt like her whole life had been leading up to this moment, to this journey into the Cotswolds.

CHAPTER TWO

Caitlyn got into her rented Volkswagen Beetle and secured her seatbelt, then she paused to look at the map again before starting the engine. Tillyhenge might not have been on GPS but it was clearly marked on the old-fashioned road map. If she just followed this road out of Meadowford-on-Smythe, took the left turn at the first intersection, got onto the A40, turned north at Burford, kept going past Shipton-Under-Wychwood and Upper Slaughter, then she should come to another intersection where—

Rap! Rap! Rap!

Caitlyn started and looked up. A pair of rheumy eyes above a long pointed nose peered at her through the glass of the driver's window. They belonged to a stooped old man dressed in a dusty black suit. He was beckoning her to get out of the car. Caitlyn hesitated a moment—the man looked a bit odd and the suit he was wearing looked like something out of the early nineteenth century, with long black tails and a white shirt with ruffled collar underneath—but it wasn't as if he was a tattooed gangster in a hoodie. Besides, he was an old man. Perhaps he was lost or needed help. She unclipped her seatbelt, opened the door, and got slowly out of the car.

"Can I help you?" she asked hesitantly.

The old man teetered to one side as he attempted to sweep her a gallant bow. He looked about a hundred years old and Caitlyn had to resist the urge to grab his elbow to prevent him from toppling over.

"I am your vampire uncle," he said, like someone turning up on your doorstep and announcing: "I'm your plumber."

"I'm sorry—what?" Caitlyn stared at him, sure that she had heard wrong.

"I am your vampire uncle," he said again, sounding slightly tetchy now.

She couldn't help it. A giggle burst from her lips.

"What is so funny?" He glared.

Caitlyn struggled to keep a straight face. "Nothing... Sorry... It's just... Well, vampires don't really exist."

"Of course, they exist!" He bristled. "There may not be so many of us left but we are still here." He scowled. "Of course, the younger ones, these days— they are too busy wasting their time on things like sparkling in the sun and falling in love... Bah!" He waved a contemptuous hand, the force of the gesture sending him teetering in the other direction. "They do not understand the important role we vampires have as Ancient Guardian Protectors. It is left to the few of us who still believe in the old ways, in duty and honour..." He puffed his bony old chest out proudly, then his brows drew together again as he saw Caitlyn's expression.

"You still do not believe me, eh? Look, I will prove it to you." He opened his jaws and pointed into his mouth. "Gooka...mai...keeghs..."

Caitlyn hesitated, then leaned forwards and peered cautiously into his sunken mouth. Before she could see anything, something fell out. She glanced down. A pair of yellowed fangs lay on the ground.

"Ah... *confounded garlic!*" cried the old man, scooping them up hastily. "These cursed fangs! That dentist swore that he had fixed them." He glowered at her. "Impossible to find a good dentist these days."

"Oh... uh... right," Caitlyn said. *Poor old dear.* He obviously had a screw loose. Several screws, it looked like. Maybe he had wandered away from a nursing home nearby? She looked around, wondering if he was with a group. Perhaps there was a seniors' outing in the village?

"So, when do we leave?"

She turned back in surprise to see the old man trying to open the car door.

"I'm sorry, I think there's a misunderstanding. I'm

not part of the tour. You need to find someone else to take you back to the nursing home."

"Nursing home? How dare you!" His pale face became suffused with colour. He drew himself to his full height. "I am Count Viktor Dracul and though I have many years on me—six hundred and thirty-four to be precise—I certainly do not require any nursing!"

Caitlyn blinked. "Er... o-kay. But you can't come with me—"

"I will not take up much room," he said. "Indeed, in my bat form, I shall occupy only a very small area of your vehicle. I can even ride in the boot if that is more convenient."

Caitlyn took a deep breath. "Look, Mr... er... Dracul—"

"You may call me Viktor... Or Uncle Viktor, if you like," he said graciously.

"Um... Right. Look, Viktor, I really can't help you. I'm not heading back to Oxford or anywhere like that. I'm going—"

"Yes, I know. You are making your way to Tillyhenge."

Caitlyn stopped and stared at him. "How did you know?"

"I have been watching, waiting for your return." He gave her a toothless smile. "I have been waiting for you a long time, Caitlyn."

"How did you know my name?" demanded Caitlyn, starting to feel creeped out.

She glanced nervously around, wondering if there

was a policeman—a local village constable—in the vicinity. Still, she felt a bit embarrassed at the thought of having to admit that she couldn't deal with one frail delusional octogenarian on her own. And besides, in spite of everything, she liked the old man. He was nuts, but he was a funny character. She didn't want to get him in trouble.

"Look... um... it's been nice chatting to you but I really need to go now," she said gently, easing between him and the car. "If you're lost, go to the tearoom at the bottom of the High Street. They're really nice in there and they'll help you get back home. Bye!"

Before he had time to respond, Caitlyn yanked the front door open, slid into the driver's seat, and slammed the door quickly after her. Then she started the engine and pulled away from the curb, driving as fast as she dared through the narrow village street.

She glanced in the rear-view mirror and breathed a sigh of relief. She'd half expected to see a scrawny old man chasing after her, his dark coat flapping behind him, but there was no one. The street behind her was empty. Caitlyn shook her head and laughed to herself. Today seemed like the day for weird things to happen.

And it's not over yet, she reminded herself as she turned onto the main road that would take her north-west, deeper into the Cotswolds, and towards Tillyhenge.

***

The drive was beautiful and Caitlyn soon found herself forgetting all about her worries as she enjoyed the scenery. It was June and the English countryside was in full bloom, with wildflowers edging the roads in a stunning array of colours: bright daisies and butter-yellow cowslips, big blue flowers of meadow cranesbill and delicate white blossoms of cow parsley, also known as Queen Anne's lace... and every so often, a burst of fuchsia from tall columns of swaying foxgloves.

Swallows swooped through the high blue sky and creamy white butterflies fluttered along the hedgerows. In fields, bordered by ancient drystone walls, cows chewed cud and ponies flicked their tails, whilst sheep grazed contentedly on sloping pastures. The car motored along winding open roads and through narrow country lanes, passing stretches where the trees spread their branches in a graceful arc overhead, turning the road into tunnels filled with dappled sunlight.

Caitlyn felt as if she was driving into another world. Her previous short visits to England had always been limited to London—Barbara Le Fey had preferred shopping, fine dining, and nightlife to rural pleasures—so Caitlyn had never had the chance to explore the English countryside. She'd heard a lot about the beauty of the rolling Cotswolds hills but she had no idea that it would be so glorious. She was so engrossed that she almost forgot about the reason for her drive. It was only when she switched on the radio for a bit of music and heard the newsreader mention the "Tillyhenge murder" that she was suddenly jolted back to reality.

"...police are still investigating the murder of Stan Matthews, local gamekeeper for the Huntingdon estate, whose body was found by the stone circle near the village of Tillyhenge. Due to the mysterious circumstances surrounding the death, the inquest has been adjourned, pending further investigation. Matthews was last seen at the local village pub just before midnight, on the night of his murder, and the police are appealing to anyone who might have information to come forward.

In other news, the Oxford City Council believes that plans for a new car park..."

Ugh. Hastily, Caitlyn switched the radio off but it was too late. The spell was broken. She remembered now that she wasn't just on a pleasant drive through the Cotswolds. In fact... she glanced at the map on the seat next to her and frowned. Surely she should have reached Tillyhenge by now? Perhaps she had overshot the turn-off for the village? She slowed as she approached an intersection, did a quick U-turn, and headed back in the direction she had come from.

She found herself almost back at the last village before she slowed the car again, biting her lip in vexation. She should have seen the turning for Tillyhenge on the way—could she have missed it again?

Making a U-turn once more, Caitlyn drove back down the same stretch of road for the third time, taking it slower and scanning the verge on either side for any sign of a turn-off. She had almost reached the intersection again and was about to give up in frustration when she saw it.

There.

An old post with a crooked wooden sign at the top and the words "Tillyhenge" etched onto the worn surface.

It stood out clearly at the side of the road, leaning over slightly. Why hadn't she seen it the previous two times? Caitlyn frowned as she turned into the narrow side road, which sloped downwards into a heavily forested valley. Trees closed in on either side and the air felt suddenly dank and cool. Caitlyn shivered as goosebumps rose on her arms; she stared through the windscreen ahead: was that a swirl of mist lying across the road?

Don't be ridiculous! She gave herself an internal shake. It was all Pomona's crazy talk stirring up her imagination. How could there be mist on the road in the middle of summer? And of course it would be cooler here in the shade, deep between the trees. *Once the road passes out of this section of forest, I'm sure things will return to normal,* Caitlyn thought as she pressed down firmly on the accelerator.

But when the road emerged at last from the thick of the woods, Caitlyn was surprised to see that the previously blue sky had turned a cloudy grey. Pomona's ominous words about the inexplicably "different" weather in Tillyhenge came back to her but she pushed the thought away. The car rolled gently down a street lined on either side with old stone cottages and came to a stop beside a large triangular patch of grass which served as the "village green". Slowly, Caitlyn got out and looked around.

Now that she was here, Tillyhenge didn't look that creepy or unusual. In fact, it looked like a dozen other little English villages featured in tourist books and travel guides. There were the winding cobbled lanes between the limestone cottages, the ancient village pub squatting proudly on one side of the village green, the quaint craft shops and local food stores, and even a few tourists wandering around, snapping shots with their cameras. The only thing missing was a church. Caitlyn scanned the surrounding rooftops but she couldn't see the familiar steeple or bell tower.

She felt slightly at loss. She had been so focused on just getting to Tillyhenge. Somehow, she had thought that all she had to do was arrive and everything would be waiting for her. Now she chided herself for being so silly. Of course it wouldn't be that easy! What had she expected? A sign welcoming her to the village, depicting a pointing hand and saying: "*Caitlyn Le Fey—answers this way*"?

She would simply have to walk around and get chatting to the locals, see if she could pick up some information. And perhaps it would be a good idea to look for a place to stay, at least for the night. Caitlyn grabbed her handbag and locked the car, then paused to rub her temples, wincing slightly. The intense concentration during the last part of the drive had given her a headache and now her head was throbbing.

She looked around again, hoping to see a pharmacy where she could pick up some painkillers. Slowly, she wandered down the widest street leading away from the village green. It looked like the "main street" in Tillyhenge, with a motley assortment of shops that included everything from an organic butcher to a traditional shoemaker. But no pharmacy.

Caitlyn rubbed her temples again, wondering whether to walk to the end of the street before turning back. A young man was coming in the opposite direction. He had a camera slung over one shoulder and at first she thought that he was a tourist. Then she realised from the size and sleek, professional look of the camera that this was no average visitor. In fact, she'd seen his air of predatory alertness before, from her experience with the paparazzi. This was a reporter on the hunt for news. Considering that there had been a recent murder in the village, it probably wasn't surprising to find the media here. Still, the last thing Caitlyn wanted was to catch their notice.

Too late. Before she could cross to the other side of the street and avoid him, the young man came up to her.

"Hey... I've been here the last few days and I haven't seen you around. You new to the village?" He gave her a cocky smile.

"Yes, I just arrived," murmured Caitlyn, trying to brush past him.

"Thought so! I would have remembered a gorgeous redhead like you," he said, giving her a wink and barring her way. "Fancy a drink at the pub?"

"No thanks," said Caitlyn, attempting to edge past him again.

"Hey, no need to be so snooty! Where're you from? You American? I think I can hear a hint of an American accent—" He narrowed his eyes suddenly and leaned closer. "Hang on a minute... do I know you? You look kind of familiar..."

Caitlyn stiffened.

The reporter snapped his fingers. "You're some kind of celebrity, aren't you? What are you doing in Tillyhenge?"

CHAPTER THREE

"I... I don't know what you're talking about," said Caitlyn, stumbling backwards.

With Barbara Le Fey's nomadic lifestyle and avoidance of celebrity socialising, Caitlyn had led a pretty quiet life, out of the public eye. She didn't think most people in the street would recognise her. But the media was a different kettle of fish. They had access to old photos and archives, and she knew they were experts at sniffing out a story. The paparazzi had been out in force at Barbara's funeral and she knew that there had been a lot of speculation about the car crash. The last thing she needed was for this reporter to recognise her and wonder what she was doing in Tillyhenge. She wouldn't put it past him to link the recent local murder with Barbara's death in some lurid way, and splash it across the front page of local papers. Anything for a story.

Quickly, she whirled and ran down the street, turning into a side lane and ducking into an open doorway. She found herself stepping into a soothing interior of warm wood and soft greens. It was some kind of natural therapy store, selling scented candles, aromatherapy oils, natural creams, and other herbal remedies.

Pomona would love it in here, thought Caitlyn, as she walked between the shelves displaying bottles of natural shampoos and organic lotions, and piles of goat milk soap, scented with English country herbs like sage, rosemary, and thyme. A soft, sweet fragrance permeated the whole store and Caitlyn felt her headache lift slightly.

"Hi! Can I help you?"

Caitlyn turned around and found herself facing a fresh-faced young girl of about eighteen, who was smiling at her eagerly.

"Um... I don't suppose you sell any paracetamol? Or aspirin?"

The girl shook her head vehemently. "Oh, no! We don't stock any of that nasty chemical stuff."

Caitlyn massaged her temples. "Oh. Well, have you got any... um... natural remedies for a headache?"

The girl looked around, then lowered her voice. "We've got some herbal balms that you can rub on your temples and there's also willow bark tea but—if you'll let me try it on you—I've got something that'll work much better."

"What's that?"

"A *Migrainus Disposa* spell! I've just learnt it and I've been practising all week."

"A what?" Caitlyn was sure she had heard wrong.

"Don't worry—you just need to close your eyes. It'll be brilliant! You'll see!"

Caitlyn hesitated but the girl was looking at her like an eager puppy and she didn't have the heart to say no. Besides, it was probably just some more New Age nonsense—like that time Pomona insisted on cleansing her aura and made Caitlyn sit in a saltwater bath for hours until she was wrinkled like a prune. It probably wouldn't do any real harm.

Obediently, Caitlyn closed her eyes. She felt the other girl's fingers lightly on her temples and heard her muttering something under her breath. The next moment, a gust of wind *whooshed* around her and Caitlyn opened her eyes in surprise.

She saw the girl staring at her in horror.

"Oh my Goddess... Okay, okay... Don't worry... I can fix it—"

"Fix what?" said Caitlyn. She groped around her temples and gasped as her fingers felt something leafy growing out of her ears. *"What have you done?"*

"Nothing that can't be fixed! It was just a small slip-up... must have got the words in the wrong order... But don't worry, I'll fix it in a jiffy! Just close your eyes again!"

She grabbed Caitlyn's ears with both hands and

yanked her head closer, then muttered some more unintelligible words under her breath. Caitlyn felt her ears go hot, then cold, and then another gust of wind envelop them. She opened her eyes to see the girl slowly opening hers too.

"GAAH!" The girl jumped backwards, clamping a hand to her mouth, her eyes on Caitlyn's face.

"What? WHAT?" said Caitlyn, starting to feel really panicked now.

She looked frantically around and spied a mirror on the wall nearby. She rushed over to take a look, then shrieked. Her eyebrows had turned into a giant monobrow, joined in the middle like a big hairy caterpillar crawling across her forehead.

She turned back to the girl. "What have you done to me?"

"I'm so sorry!" cried the girl, wringing her hands. "But don't worry—there's no need to panic. I can fix it. I just need to do a spell to reverse it... Now, was it *'Frown begone, brow unjoin'*? Or was it *'Frown begone, brow undone'*? Maybe I should—"

"EVIE!"

The girl cringed as a plump, middle-aged woman dressed in a bright purple kaftan hurried up to them. Her frizzy red hair peeked out from beneath a purple turban, and her eyes were framed by purple wire-rimmed spectacles, but her eccentric appearance was belied by her kindly face. She looked at Caitlyn in horror.

"What have you done to the customer?" she

demanded.

The girl stammered, "N-nothing, Mum... She... she had a headache and... well, I was trying out—"

"Evie, what did I tell you about performing spells on the customers?" the woman said severely. "If she had a headache, why didn't you just give her the Peppermint & Lavender Soothing Head Balm? Or the Willow Bark Tea?"

"Well, magic works so much better..." Evie said sullenly.

"Not when you don't know how to use it," the woman snapped. "You could have shrunk her head or even blown her up!"

"Er... I'm still standing here, you know," said Caitlyn, raising her hand.

The woman turned back to her with a bright smile. "Oh, yes! Hello, dear. I'm Bertha and this is my daughter, Evie. Welcome to *Herbal Enchantments*. We stock a range of products made from the finest natural ingredients, based on traditional English remedies that have been handed down through generations."

Caitlyn stared incredulously as the woman continued beaming at her. "Uh... that's great. But what about my eyebrows?" She looked at Bertha anxiously. "You'll be able to fix this, right? I won't have to go around with a monobrow for the rest of my life?"

"Hmm? Oh, oh yes, of course..." Bertha snapped her fingers. "*Visago Revertus!*"

Caitlyn felt a whirl of air around her and something scraped across her forehead. She rushed back to the mirror and sighed in relief. Her eyebrows were back to normal.

"Now, let me give you something for that headache," added Bertha with a smile.

"Oh no, no, that's okay," said Caitlyn hastily. "Thanks all the same but I've got to go now—"

Somehow, a small tray had appeared on the counter next to them. Bertha lifted a teapot from the tray and poured some steaming liquid into a mug, which she handed to Caitlyn.

"Drink this."

Caitlyn hesitated. The last thing she wanted to do was try anything else from this store. But Bertha's kindly face and air of quiet authority invited trust. Cupping the mug in her hands, Caitlyn raised it to her lips and sipped carefully. The drink had an unusual flavour she had never tasted before but it was quite pleasant, with an earthy aroma. She took a few bigger gulps, then looked back up.

"It's willow bark tea," Bertha said in answer to Caitlyn's silent question. "It's an old traditional remedy for headaches. Feel better?"

Caitlyn started to give a fake polite answer, then stopped in surprise. Actually, she *did* feel better. In fact, her headache had completely lifted!

"My headache's gone!"

"Good." The older woman smiled, then looked at her curiously. "Are you visiting Tillyhenge?"

"Yes. I just arrived."

"And where are you from?"

"Um... well, my... uh... my mother was American, although we hardly lived there. She was a singer and we moved around a lot, lived in different countries."

"Really?" The other woman kept looking strangely at her until Caitlyn began to wonder if something else was growing out of her head.

"Is something the matter?" she asked at last.

"Oh no. It's just that... well, you look a lot like... someone I used to know." The older woman blinked and shook her head. "Perhaps it's my imagination."

The other woman's staring was making Caitlyn uncomfortable and she hurried to change the subject. "Um... I don't suppose you know of a place I could stay for the night? Is there an inn or bed and breakfast in the village?"

"No," said Bertha regretfully. "The only place that has rooms to board is the pub but I believe both their rooms are taken. We don't normally get many visitors to stay in Tillyhenge..."

"There's Grandma's place!" Evie spoke up. "She's got that attic bedroom, remember? We were telling her she should let it for some money."

"Hmm..." Bertha looked unsure. "Well, I suppose..."

"Does your mother have a house nearby?" Caitlyn asked.

"A shop, actually. She lives at the back of the shop herself, but she does have an empty room upstairs."

31

"Oh, that's great! Can you give me directions to her place?"

Bertha hesitated again and Caitlyn looked at her curiously. Why was she so reluctant? It was almost as if she was nervous about something.

Bertha frowned. "Maybe I ought to come with you—explain things to Mother…"

There was a bustling in the doorway of the store and two tourists came in. Evie went eagerly towards them and Bertha glanced anxiously after her.

"You'd better go and look after your customers," said Caitlyn hastily, not wanting others to suffer the same fate she had under Evie's hands.

Bertha hesitated again, then sighed and said quickly, "It's the chocolate shop at the edge of the village. Take the street opposite the pub, from the village green, and follow it to the old water pump, then take a left and then a right, and you'll find yourself on a narrow lane leading out of the village. The chocolate shop is at the end of that lane."

"Thanks." Caitlyn gave her a wave and left the store.

She went back to her car to retrieve her overnight bag, then followed the directions to find the chocolate shop. On the way, she mulled over what had just happened in *Herbal Enchantments*. How had Evie managed to make those things grow out of her ears? And fuse her eyebrows? And how had Bertha changed her eyebrows back to normal? It must have been some kind of prank, Caitlyn decided. Like an elaborate hoax. The gust of air could have been done with an electric fan. And maybe Evie had stuck something on Caitlyn's forehead when her eyes were shut... or maybe... maybe the *mirror* was rigged to show a fake image... Yes, that must have been it. And all that talk of spells... well, it was probably all part of the hoax, the kind of thing you said to hook gullible tourists...

It couldn't really have been magic... because magic didn't exist, right?

Caitlyn realised that she had been walking around in circles for a while and still hadn't found the chocolate shop. For a tiny village, Tillyhenge sure had a lot of winding lanes and alleys, all twisting together like a rabbit warren. She had lost all sense of direction now and wasn't even sure she could find her way back to the village green. Then to her relief, she saw an elderly lady coming towards her, pulling a wheelie shopping trolley behind her.

"Excuse me, can you tell me the way to the chocolate shop?"

The old woman gave her a look of fear. "You don't want to eat anything from there!"

"Oh, no, I'm not interested in the chocolates," Caitlyn explained. "I just need a place to—"

"I wouldn't touch anything from the Widow Mags! Not if you paid me all the money in China!" The woman hurried off, her shopping trolley rattling behind her.

Caitlyn watched her go, bewildered. Then she

spied two more figures walking towards her. They were a mother and a little girl of about six years old. The woman gave her a friendly smile as she approached.

"Excuse me, do you know the way to the chocolate shop?"

The woman's face changed. "The chocolate shop?"

"Yes, I was told that there might be a room there. I need somewhere to stay for the night."

The little girl tugged her mother's hand urgently. "No, Mummy! Don't let her go to the chocolate shop! The witch lives there!"

"Hush!" the woman admonished. She looked back up at Caitlyn with an embarrassed smile. "Er... perhaps it would be better for you to find another place to stay. I don't think the chocolate shop is the most... er... hospitable."

"Oh. Well, is there anywhere else in the village you can recommend? I was told the pub is fully booked."

The woman gave her a regretful look. "Sorry. Yes, you're right—the only other option is the pub and the reporter and that South African gentleman are staying there. I suppose you'd have to go to the next village?"

Caitlyn bit her lip. She was tired and didn't want to drive anywhere else that day. Besides, after all the trouble she'd taken to find Tillyhenge, she was loathe to leave again so soon.

She gave the woman a determined smile. "I'm sure the chocolate shop will be fine for one night. Can you please tell me how to get there?"

Reluctantly, the woman turned and pointed down the street, giving Caitlyn directions.

"What's the shop called?" asked Caitlyn.

The woman hesitated, then said, "*Bewitched by Chocolate.*"

"Oh!" Caitlyn smiled. "That's a lovely name."

"Er, yes…" The woman looked uncomfortable.

"Have you tried any of the chocolates?"

"Once." The woman looked scared. "They… they taste amazing. Almost too good to be real. You wonder what the Widow Mags puts in them."

Grabbing her child's hand, she turned and hurried away. Caitlyn stared after her. In her mind's eye, she suddenly saw Pomona again, sitting across the table from her back at the tearoom in Meadowford… and her cousin eagerly reading the tea leaves and telling her that there would be "chocolate" in her future… Her spine tingled. Then, brushing the memory away, she began making her way to the chocolate shop at the edge of the village.

CHAPTER FOUR

Caitlyn looked up at the shop in front of her. *Bewitched by Chocolate* was housed in a traditional Cotswold cottage, but unlike the cottages usually seen in postcards and travel guides, with their glowing honey-coloured stone walls and pretty thatched roofs, the walls on this one were crumbling, with a greyish-green tinge, and the thatched roof looked ragged and sagging. The windows were dark and covered with cobwebs, and the front doorway yawned like an open mouth, dark and foreboding.

Caitlyn shivered, rubbing her arms. She hadn't seen a place look less inviting. Did she really want to spend a night here? Wasn't she better to drive on and find a B&B in another village?

Just as she was about to turn away, something wafted out of the doorway of the shop. Caitlyn froze in her tracks as the wonderful rich aroma of chocolate filled her senses. Dark, sweet, and heavenly, Caitlyn could almost taste the creamy confection melting on her tongue. Her mouth started watering. Almost against her will, she stepped through the darkened doorway and walked inside.

Slowly her eyes grew accustomed to the darkened interior and she looked around in wonder. The place was like Aladdin's cave—if Aladdin's cave had been filled with gourmet chocolates and cocoa delights, instead of gold and jewels. Boxes of crunchy, chocolate-coated nougat and soft, buttery caramels filled the alcoves in the walls, next to smooth, creamy fudges and jars of rich chocolate sauce. Solid chocolate bars in milk, dark and white chocolate decorated the shelves, their smooth surfaces topped with crispy cocoa nibs, whole almonds, zesty orange peels, and crunchy toffee pieces.

On the counter that ran along the back wall were various bowls of cocoa-dusted chocolate beans and succulent chocolate-dipped apricots and strawberries. And beneath the counter, just visible under the dusty glass pane, was an array of chocolate truffles and luscious bonbons, gleaming and oozing with delectable flavours.

The shop seemed empty, however. Caitlyn frowned as she approached the counter, wondering where the Widow Mags was. There was a small alcove behind the counter—what was obviously the original hearth fireplace—and Caitlyn was surprised to see a cast-iron cauldron hanging over an open fire, filled with a dark molten liquid that was bubbling away merrily. *Chocolate.* Caitlyn inhaled deeply. Yes, the whole shop smelled amazing but that cauldron was the source of the most incredible aroma of rich, dark chocolate.

Suddenly, a dark shape heaved up from behind the counter. Caitlyn caught a glimpse of a hunched back, wild grey hair and a large hooked nose. She jumped and screamed.

The old woman behind the counter yelped and jumped too, sending cocoa beans flying everywhere. They scattered across the counter and rolled onto the floor.

"What are you doing, girl? You scared me half to death!" the old woman snapped.

Caitlyn choked. "*Me?* Scare *you?*"

"Yes, what was all that screaming for?"

"You just appeared out of nowhere and I thought you were a wi—" Caitlyn bit off the word just in time. "Uh... I guess you just startled me."

She leaned back and took a better look at the Widow Mags. She realised that the hunchback impression was due to a dowager's hump—something a lot of older women with osteoporosis were prone to—and the wild grey hair was simply wispy ends that had come loose from the bun at the nape of the old woman's neck. Her nose was quite large and hooked, yes, but the thing that had looked like a wart on the end was actually a blob of chocolate, dried into a funny shape.

In fact, on closer inspection, the Widow Mags looked like nothing more than an old woman with a faded shawl around her shoulders and skinny chicken legs peeking out from beneath the hem of her ragged black dress. A grumpy old woman, at that. She was scowling now as she peered at Caitlyn from beneath her wrinkled brow.

"What are you staring at?"

"Oh, n-nothing," said Caitlyn, hastily averting her eyes.

The old woman growled, "If you want to buy some chocolates, hurry up and tell me what you want!"

Good grief. No wonder there was no one in the store. The old woman's customer service manner seriously needed work.

"Actually, I'm not here about the chocolates. I came to ask—" Caitlyn broke off as she saw the Widow Mags stoop painfully to collect the spilled cocoa beans. The old woman fumbled as her gnarled hands—the fingers stiff with arthritis—struggled to grip the beans and pick them up.

"Here, let me help you," said Caitlyn, dropping to the floor beside her.

"I can manage!" the old woman snarled.

Taken aback, Caitlyn was tempted to stand up and leave the cranky old biddy to her own devices. Then she felt a wave of compassion. She recognised pride when she saw it: like many senior citizens who had once been proudly independent, the Widow Mags was having a hard time now that she was getting older and could no longer do the things she used to. She needed help but didn't know how to ask for it—or even how to receive it graciously.

Caitlyn took a deep breath and smiled at the old woman. "Yes, I'm sure you can—but I'd still like to help."

The Widow Mags hesitated, then said, "Well, fine... Make sure you don't miss the small ones."

Quickly, Caitlyn picked up all the spilled cocoa beans and returned them to the bowl.

The Widow Mags mumbled, "Thank you... not that I couldn't have done it myself, mind you."

Caitlyn stifled a laugh, wondering if anyone had ever been thanked so grudgingly.

The old woman flung an awkward hand towards the display of truffles beneath the counter. "Have a taste of my chocolates."

"Oh, no, that's okay. I wasn't expecting—"

"Choose a chocolate!" snarled the old woman.

Quickly, Caitlyn grabbed a chocolate truffle and stuffed it into her mouth. Whatever negative feelings she might have felt towards the old woman disappeared as soon as the truffle melted on her tongue. She closed her eyes in ecstasy. A velvety soft ganache cream centre, blended with buttery caramel, covered with rich dark chocolate and dusted all over with pure cocoa. *Heaven.*

Caitlyn opened her eyes. "That... that was incredible! What did you put in it?"

"What do you mean? Are you suggesting that I spike my chocolates with something?" demanded the old woman.

"No, no, it's just that they're so delicious! I've never tasted chocolates like these—and believe me, I've eaten a *lot* of chocolates."

The old woman's face softened. "*Harrumph...* well, thank you," she said gruffly.

Caitlyn gave her a smile. "I'd love to buy some to give my cousin—can I get a box made up?"

The old woman softened even further. "Of course. Which ones would you like?"

Caitlyn looked down helplessly at the rows and rows of gorgeous truffles and chocolate bonbons. She had no idea how to choose—they all looked delicious.

"Taste them," the Widow Mags suggested. "That's the best way to choose."

"Okay," said Caitlyn, not about to turn down an offer to have more chocolate! "But you must let me pay for the ones I taste as well," she insisted.

The old woman didn't answer, but nodded again towards the display. Caitlyn began selecting various pieces at random and popping them in her mouth, sighing with pleasure as the rich creamy flavours melted on her tongue.

There was a velvety chocolate ganache with freshly-roasted, chopped hazelnuts, covered in a crisp milk chocolate coating... a dark chocolate truffle cup infused with fragrant Madagascar vanilla... a cluster of crunchy English toffee dipped in hand-made dark chocolate... a creamy milk chocolate shell with a salty-sweet peanut butter centre... a refreshing white chocolate truffle with a zesty lemon ganache centre topped with a candied lemon slice... followed by an intense espresso truffle cup filled with mocha ganache and decorated with dark chocolate shavings...

Her appetite was going to be completely ruined for dinner but Caitlyn didn't care. She felt like her head was swimming with the amazingly rich, intense flavours of the chocolates that she had eaten.

"How many is that?" she asked at last. So far, she had picked every single one she had tasted.

"Twelve," said the Widow Mags.

"Okay, I'll take two of each and make up a box of twenty-four. Pomie's going to go *mad* for these."

As the Widow Mags began filling up a shallow box tray, Caitlyn heard a step behind her and turned to see two figures hovering in the doorway of the chocolate shop. She recognised them as a couple of tourists she had seen earlier on the village green. They were peering into the dim interior, looking uncertainly around.

Impulsively, Caitlyn stepped forward and gave them a warm smile. "Come in! Come in and have a look around."

The couple came in, responding to her smile with ones of their own.

"My wife and I were wandering through the village and came down this lane. We could smell this wonderful—"

"Oh, you must try some of these chocolates!" said Caitlyn, grabbing the half-filled box of chocolates out of the Widow Mags's hands and thrusting them in front of the tourists. The man and his wife looked down at the truffles, their faces brightening. They each selected one and Caitlyn watched their eyes glaze over as the delicious flavours hit them.

"Oh, these are absolutely divine!" cried the wife. "Ralph, we've got to get some for the girls!"

"How much are they?" asked the husband, greedily helping himself to another.

Caitlyn threw a glance at the Widow Mags who was looking dumbfounded, and blurted, "We're doing a special at the moment. Three for the price of two."

"That sounds like a great deal," said the husband. "We'll take six boxes."

Caitlyn glanced at the Widow Mags again. The old woman was staring, open-mouthed. Hastily, Caitlyn slipped behind the counter herself and took the tongs from the old woman's nerveless fingers. Quickly, she filled up six boxes of chocolates, while the couple browsed around the shop. By the time they left, they'd also bought several chocolate bars, a bag of chocolate-dipped strawberries, and a jar of decadent chocolate sauce.

Caitlyn felt a ridiculous sense of pride watching them carry their purchases out the shop, then she remembered belatedly that it wasn't her store. She looked uncertainly at the old woman.

"Er… I hope I didn't step out of line, offering that special deal. I know you didn't really have one but I just thought—"

"That was more money than I've made all week," murmured the Widow Mags, looking gobsmacked. Then she added quickly, "But you must take half of it for your efforts—"

"No!" said Caitlyn, taking a step backwards. "No, no, I won't accept anything. It was no big deal and it was fun." She gave the old woman a smile. "I've… uh… never really had a job and it's nice to… well, to feel a sense of achievement." She paused, then hurried on, "But there *is* something you could do for me in return, if you really want to thank me."

The Widow Mags looked at her questioningly.

"I'm looking for somewhere to stay and your daughter, Bertha, told me that you might have a room to rent?"

The old woman scowled. "That Bertha. Meddling in my business again. Always fussing over me and worrying about me. I told her I was managing fine—I didn't need her to pay my last electric bill! And now she's going around touting my home out like a bloody bed and breakfast. *Humph!*"

"But it does seem silly to waste the chance of earning some money when you're not using the room anyway," Caitlyn pointed out. Then she remembered the old woman's pride and added quickly, "And it would be doing me a big favour…?" She trailed off hopefully.

"It's very basic. Nothing fancy," the Widow Mags growled.

She led Caitlyn through a doorway behind the counter and into a small hallway behind the main shop area, with three doors leading off in different directions. Straight in front was an open doorway to an enormous kitchen; to the left a closed door led to what was obviously the Widow Mags's private quarters; and on the right, another open doorway showed a narrow spiral staircase curving upwards. The Widow Mags pointed to this:

"Up the spiral staircase. Take a look yourself."

Caitlyn climbed the circling steps and found herself on a small landing which led into an attic bedroom with sloping ceilings and a tiny dormer window. A single brass bed stood in one corner, next to an old chest of drawers with a chipped washbasin and old-fashioned water jug stacked on the end. A wooden chair with crooked legs was the only other furniture in the room.

A door on the landing opposite the bedroom led into a cramped bathroom. Caitlyn turned the taps at the cracked porcelain sink. Rusty brown water gushed out, taking several minutes to run clear. She tested it with her fingers. The water was icy cold. She swallowed and shut the taps, then went back to survey the room. "Basic" was right. She had never stayed anywhere as rustic as this—but she wasn't going to allow herself to be daunted. A bit of dust and cold water never hurt anyone, right?

She walked over to the window, opened it, and looked out. The room faced the back of the shop, with a view of the empty expanse of hill behind the cottage. A stretch of forest hugged one side of the hill, starting from the edge of the cottage backyard and following the slope upwards until it reached the top of the hill, where the slope met the horizon.

Caitlyn took a deep breath of the fresh country air and smiled to herself. Rough and basic as it was, there was something homely about the room and she found herself feeling strangely at peace. Giving the view a last look, she turned and headed back down to tell the Widow Mags that she had a new lodger.

CHAPTER FIVE

Caitlyn moaned in her sleep and moved restlessly. The air was hot and stifling, and her legs tangled in the blankets as she thrashed around in the bed.

Then suddenly, she was awake. She sat up, breathing quickly. She had been dreaming of fire: vivid orange flames crackling with heat and licking their way towards her, threatening to engulf her...

Caitlyn gave her head a sharp shake. It was a dream, that was all. *Probably the result of eating too much chocolate*, she thought with a wry smile. She lifted the blankets away, grimacing slightly. She was drenched in sweat. Sighing, she pushed back the covers, then made as if to lie down again. But her gaze went to the open window. She could see light flickering on the bedroom wall next to the window and realised that the source was coming from outside.

Curious, Caitlyn padded over to the window and peered out. She had left it open before going to bed, because of the warm night, and now she leaned out as far as she dared to look around. She could see nothing in the dark shadows around the back of the cottage, but in the distance, at the top of the hill, was an orange-crimson glow which lit up the night sky.

Caitlyn frowned. Someone had built a fire on the hill—and not just any small campfire either. No, that kind of glow had to be coming from a huge bonfire. She glanced at the clock on the wall behind her. It was just past midnight. Who on earth was out there in the Cotswolds hills, building a bonfire in the middle of the night?

A breath of air came through the window, bringing with it a faint smell of smoke. And was that music she could hear, almost imperceptibly, on the wind? Caitlyn strained her ears. No, perhaps it had been her imagination. She stared at the glow on the horizon for a moment longer—it seemed to be ebbing now; the fire was dying, perhaps it had been put out—then she eased herself back into the room and shut the window firmly behind her. It would be hotter and more airless without the window open but she felt better having some sort of barrier between herself and the dark wilderness outside.

Walking back to the bed, Caitlyn stripped off the blankets and lay down on top of the sheets. She closed her eyes, although she didn't think she'd be able to go back to sleep. In her mind's eye, she kept seeing that orange glow on the horizon, flickering and shifting like a living thing. *Who would build a bonfire in the middle of the night and why? Was it some kind of gathering?* She couldn't help remembering Pomona's words about Tillyhenge and the strange rumours surrounding this village. It was just the kind of place where she could imagine pagan rituals still taking place...

The next time Caitlyn opened her eyes, it was morning. She sat up slowly, rubbing her eyes, surprised that she had fallen asleep again after all. Her gaze went to the window and she got up and flung it open. What she saw was a perfectly normal view of the English countryside, with everything looking just the way it had when she first looked out yesterday. An early morning breeze rustled through the trees and she heard cows mooing softly in the distance.

Caitlyn scanned the horizon. There was nothing— no wisps of smoke or any other sign of a fire. She rubbed her eyes again. Had she dreamt the whole thing? Feeling slightly silly, Caitlyn retreated from the window. She washed as thoroughly as she could in the tiny bathroom, gasping as the icy water stung her skin, then she put on fresh clothes and hurried downstairs. The chocolate store was still closed, and when she knocked on the door leading to the Widow Mags's private quarters, she got no answer.

Caitlyn hesitated, then wandered into the kitchen.

She noticed that the rear door was unlocked—perhaps the Widow Mags had gone out for a walk in the woods behind the cottage? Anyway, she could find the old woman later. For now, she wanted to get some breakfast. Making up her mind, she turned and went out the front of the chocolate shop. She would head to the village green and hunt down the local bakery. Her stomach was rumbling and she couldn't have chocolate for breakfast—although she was sorely tempted!

The first store Caitlyn encountered was the village post shop, a few doors down from the pub. She stepped inside and found that it was filled with a large group of middle-aged women gathered around the postmistress, who was standing behind the counter by the cash machine. They had their heads together, obviously busily gossiping.

"... it's Matthews's wife, I'm sure it is," said the postmistress, nodding knowledgeably.

"Amy Matthews? She's a little mouse! I can't imagine her killing her husband!" a woman with a purple rinse cried.

The postmistress shook her head. "It's the quiet ones that are the worst."

A large woman with an ample bosom put a hand on her hips. "Well, I, for one, wouldn't be surprised if his wife murdered him. Did you know that he was beating her? I saw her the other day, with a bruise the size of Africa on one side of her face. Tried to tell me she walked into a door—hah! I know the signs of domestic abuse when I see it. Matthews had a foul temper when he was drunk."

"They think he was poisoned, don't they? She could have slipped something in his supper—"

"Where would she have got the poison, though? It was an extract from a herb, wasn't it?"

"Belladonna, they call it. Grows really easily around here."

The postmistress nodded. "Yes, and I've seen it growing in *one* particular garden."

"You have?"

"Where?"

"Down behind the chocolate shop."

Gasps. "The chocolate shop! You mean, the Widow Mags?"

"I always knew there was something evil about that woman," said the woman with the purple rinse.

"Yes, me too! They say she's a witch—she and that batty daughter and granddaughter of hers, who run the herbal store."

"We ought to tell the police."

"What, tell the police that she's a witch? They'd never believe us. They think she's just a harmless old woman."

"Harmless old woman? Have you seen those chocolates of hers? Enchanted by the devil, they are!" said the woman with the large bosom.

More gasps. "Really? How do you know?"

"I tasted them, didn't I? There's no way on earth they could taste that good, not unless there's magic in 'em. Dark magic, if you ask me."

"Oh my goodness, yes, I had some once too and they made me feel... oh, I can't describe it but it was downright sinful!"

The postmistress leaned forwards. "Well, like I said, I've gone into the cottage garden a few times when no one was looking—not that I was sneaking around or anything, of course—and I saw, with my own eyes, belladonna plants growing there, bold as you please! And I'll tell you something else. I saw Amy Matthews down at the chocolate shop several times in the last month. Thick as thieves, those two are. I wouldn't be surprised if the Widow Mags is involved..."

"Do you think she cast a spell on him?"

A new woman spoke up in the group: "My nephew went up with the other men of the village to help bring the body back. He told me that Stan Matthews was stiff as a board, with his body all contorted and his fingers curled up like claws. And his eyes! They were open and staring and black as night. Stan Matthews had blue eyes—but when they found him, his eyes were black."

Gasps and shudders all around the circle.

"Witchcraft! It has to be!"

"Oh my..."

"Fair gives you the shivers, it does!"

"I heard that—" the postmistress broke off as she looked up and saw Caitlyn. "Oh, hullo, miss! What can I do for you?"

The talking ceased as everyone turned to look at Caitlyn. She flushed slightly under their unabashed stares. She knew that life in these small villages revolved around finding fodder for gossip and, as a newcomer, she was "fresh meat" for all those poking noses and wagging tongues.

"Oh... um... I was hoping to pick up some breakfast..."

"The bakery's just around the corner," said the postmistress. "I'm afraid we don't stock any fresh baking here. We do have milk and you can buy a bottle and have it with some cereal, if you like. All the cereals and biscuits are down there." She indicated the aisle next to the counter.

"Thanks... I think I'll get something from the bakery. But while I'm here, I might take a look around..." Caitlyn wandered down the aisle, marvelling at the range of things on the shelves. Like many village post shops, the place was tiny and yet crammed with goods, selling everything from postcards to pasta, toothpaste to wine, USB sticks, gardening gloves, local cheeses, dry-cleaning, fresh flowers, maps...

"Are you looking for something in particular, miss?" asked the postmistress, leaning over the counter to watch her.

Caitlyn smiled. "Oh, no... not really. I'm just browsing."

"You American, miss?" one of the women spoke up.

Caitlyn hesitated. She didn't feel like giving the long answer. "Um... yes, sort of."

The other women pressed forwards eagerly, questions tumbling out of their mouths.

"Which part of America, miss?"

"Er... my mother's from California. But I... I didn't really live there much myself."

"Where did you live?" another asked.

"Um... all over the world really. My... um... my family moved around a lot."

"Got brothers and sisters, have you?"

"No, I'm an only child."

Several women shook their heads, clucking their tongues. "Aww... now that's a shame. Must have been lonely growing up."

Caitlyn smiled wanly. "I managed okay. I have a cousin that I'm really close to."

"You travelling alone, then? No nice young man?" One woman gave her a coy look.

"No," said Caitlyn, slightly taken aback at her nosiness.

"Well, plenty of time for that. Maybe you'll find a nice British chap." Another coy look.

"Er..."

"You sure you're American?" said the postmistress with a chuckle. "Funny—you don't sound like the other American tourists. Your accent... it sounds a bit English to my ears, although you say some words the American way..."

"Oh, I had a British nanny growing up—I was

home-schooled and I spent most of my time with her. I guess I picked up her accent." Caitlyn hesitated, then taking a deep breath, she added, "And actually, I was born in England. In this area."

"In the Cotswolds?" Several eyebrows shot up. Caitlyn saw the women practically perk up their ears, like foxhounds who had scented a rabbit. They all eyed her with avid curiosity.

Caitlyn nodded, then she added casually, "By the way, I've been hearing a lot about a stone circle near the village?"

The postmistress nodded. "One of our local attractions, it is."

"I'd love to see it—is it easy to get to?" asked Caitlyn.

"It's up the hill at the south end of the village, miss," said the postmistress. "You go down the lane by the water pump and when you get to the bottom, you'll see a chocolate shop. Go round that and up the hill behind it. The stones are at the top of that hill, just on the edge of the woods."

"Oh!" Caitlyn stared at her. "I think I know—in fact, I think someone was lighting a bonfire there last night."

The women went still. The atmosphere in the room changed.

Caitlyn looked at them curiously. "Did any of you see it?"

"A fire, you say?" said the postmistress with forced indifference. "Can't say I've heard anything about it.

Are you sure you weren't mistaken?"

"Yes, I saw it from my bedroom window. I'm staying at the chocolate shop and my room faces the hill and the woods behind the cottage. I woke up in the middle of the night and saw the glow on the horizon. It was just after midnight." Caitlyn looked at the woman closest to her. "It had to have been a large bonfire—I wondered if it was it some kind of special gathering?"

"I don't know what you're talking about, miss," said the woman, avoiding her gaze. The rest of the women shifted uncomfortably and several began whispering to each other.

"I think you must have imagined it," said the postmistress. "Perhaps it was a dream and you woke up confused... That happens to me sometimes. Why, I remember once when I was on holiday down in Bournemouth—"

"No, I saw it," insisted Caitlyn. "It was exactly where you say the stone circle is. In fact, aren't stone circles believed to be places of powerful magic? Perhaps it was some kind of pagan folk ritual—"

"I've never heard of anything like that around here," interrupted the postmistress.

"No, certainly not," said the other woman firmly.

The atmosphere was decidedly chilly now and several of the women were eyeing her in an almost hostile manner.

"Oh." Caitlyn looked around the group of women. She was puzzled by their manner. They had seemed so chatty, so interested in her background... then she realised that it was the mention of the mysterious bonfire that had made them clam up. *Why?*

She cleared her throat. "Um... well, perhaps you're right and I did imagine it." She gave them all a bright smile. "I'll head on over to the bakery now. It was nice meeting you."

Turning, she walked slowly out of the store, conscious of the eyes boring into her back as she stepped out into the street.

CHAPTER SIX

Caitlyn entered the village bakery and her heart sank as she saw another group of women there—younger women this time—their heads together, talking furtively. Did the women in this village do nothing else besides gossip?

The baker glanced up from the dough he was kneading behind the counter and dusted the flour off his hands.

"What can I get for you, miss?"

Caitlyn looked at him hopefully. She was desperate for a cup of coffee. "Do you do coffee?"

He shook his head. "Sorry, luv. Don't serve drinks in here."

"Oh, okay. Well, I'll just buy something to eat first then." Caitlyn approached the large display shelves next to the counter. It was a simple bakery, with no fancy pastries or cakes. There were country grain cobs and rustic loaves, accompanied by a few sweet buns and fruit loafs, as well as some savoury meat pies and sausage rolls. Caitlyn bought a Chelsea bun and bit into it eagerly as soon as the baker handed it to her in a paper bag. It was slightly stodgy and the cinnamon flavour was weak, but she was so hungry that she didn't care.

As she ate the bun, she couldn't help hearing the tittering conversation behind her. It seemed like there was only one topic of conversation in the village: the women were busily speculating about the murder.

"... do you think the police have any suspects?"

"I passed Lord Fitzroy speaking to the inspector yesterday, down by the village green. It sounded like they'd just finished interviewing that South African chap. Hans Something-or-Other."

"You don't suppose he did it, Angela?"

"Oh no, my money's on the wife. I always thought there was something funny about her. Looks all sweet and innocent, all 'butter-wouldn't-melt-in-her-mouth'... but I'll bet she's a filthy little tart inside."

Caitlyn turned, slightly shocked, to look at the speaker, the one called "Angela". She was a tall woman in her early thirties with an upturned nose and overly-styled, bottle blonde hair. She wore a fashionable shirt dress, belted at the waist, and was attractive in a superficial way, although her looks were marred by her sneering smile and the malice in her pale blue eyes.

She leaned towards the other women and said, "And I'll bet that Amy Matthews had help. Everyone knows she's been spending time with that old woman at the chocolate shop—the witch. I think she got the Widow Mags to help her get rid of her husband."

The other women squealed in delight.

"Do you think so?"

"Ooh, Angela, that's—"

The door to the bakery opened and someone stepped in. The conversation ceased as suddenly as if someone had pressed a "Mute" button. Caitlyn glanced up. The new arrival was also a young woman in her early thirties, but very different to Angela. She was soft and pretty in that "fair English rose" kind of way. Her pale blonde hair hung loose around her shoulders and she was dressed in a simple cotton dress that, although slightly dated, flattered her slim figure. But the thing which drew Caitlyn's eye was the ugly bruise on the side of her face. It was just turning from purple to a yellowy-green and looked very painful.

"Oh my goodness, what happened to you?" blurted Caitlyn before she could stop herself.

The young woman flushed. She fiddled with her hair, trying to bring it forward to hide the bruise. "Nothing. I... I had a slight accident, that's all."

There was a burst of sniggering from the group of women behind them and the young woman flushed even more. She hurried up to the counter and said to the baker:

"Can I have one of your granary loaves, please? And two of the fruit rolls as well."

The baker wrapped up her purchases, then rang up the till and held out his hand for the money. The young woman groped in her pockets, then went pale.

"Oh! Um... I-I'm sorry... I think I might have left my purse at home. Could you keep these aside for me and I'll come back later with the money—"

"You know, we're honest folk in this village, Mrs Matthews," a voice called out. It was the tall woman named Angela. She gave a contemptuous sniff. "We don't go around asking for things without paying for it."

The young woman went bright red. "I'm sorry... I do have the money, really! It's in my purse... I just left it at home... oh, I—"

"Here, let me pay for it," Caitlyn spoke up. Angela's hostile attitude towards the young woman annoyed her, not to mention the malicious twittering from the other women in the background. She pulled out a few notes and pushed them across the counter.

The young woman turned to her. "Oh no! No, you mustn't! I can't let you—"

"Don't worry, it's only a few pounds. Honestly." Caitlyn gave her a friendly smile. "In return, perhaps you could tell me where I might get a cup of coffee?" She gave a self-deprecating laugh. "I guess I'm more of a city girl than I thought. I need my morning caffeine."

The young woman hesitated, then gave Caitlyn a shy smile. "Actually, my house is just around the corner... If you'd like to come back with me, I'd love to make a cup for you?"

"You're on!" said Caitlyn impulsively.

She didn't really know why she was going off to have coffee with a stranger but there was something about the young woman that she warmed to. *This must be Amy Matthews, the murdered gamekeeper's wife*, she realised. And from the look of that bruise, it seemed that the gossip in the post shop was right—Matthews *had* been beating his wife. Which certainly gave her a strong motive for wanting him dead... but somehow, Caitlyn couldn't believe that this timid girl in front of her could be a murderer.

They left the bakery together, ignoring the stony stares from Angela and her friends, and walked through the village to a small cottage on a side street. The place was cramped but scrupulously clean and an attempt had been made to make it as cosy as possible. There were hand-knitted rugs and cushion covers on the faded old couch and some framed photos arranged on the windowsill, including one showing a swarthy-looking man holding a shotgun which Caitlyn assumed to be of Stan Matthews.

A burst of colour came from the vase of wildflowers standing on the sideboard, next to a floor-to-ceiling bookshelf that was filled with books. Caitlyn was surprised. Somehow, from what she had heard of the gamekeeper, she didn't think he'd be the type of man to read much. Perhaps it was his wife who was the bookworm?

"Wow, you must be a great reader," said Caitlyn with a smile, gesturing to the bookshelf.

"Oh, actually, most of those aren't ours. The bookshelf was here in the house when we moved in. I've added a few books of my own but it's been great having all these other titles to choose from. I don't get much free time but when I do, I love reading."

"Me too," said Caitlyn, eyeing the bookshelf with envy. Some of the volumes on the top shelf looked almost antique, with leather-bound covers and gold engraving along the spine.

"Please take a seat," said Amy Matthews, giving her a shy smile and indicating the couch. "How do you like your coffee? With milk? Sugar?"

"Black, one sugar please," said Caitlyn.

As the gamekeeper's wife disappeared into the kitchen, Caitlyn wandered over to the bookshelf, unable to resist its allure. She ran her fingers along the spines, pulling out a few at random. Then she paused as she pulled out a slim book entitled *Myths and Legends of Tillyhenge*. It looked like an amateur publication—something a local historical association might have put together, maybe for the tourists. She flipped it open and her eyes devoured the words on the page:

There are many stone circles and standing stones

around the British Isles, including Stonehenge, the famous site which has fascinated people for centuries. But equally mysterious is our very own stone circle here on the outskirts of the village of Tillyhenge. Believed by some to be the frozen forms of medieval warriors turned to stone by a sinister spell, it is said that they awaken each night at the witching hour and return to their human form—however, any who dare lay eyes on them during this time will be blinded forever.

Other legends speak of the power of the stones and the dangerous consequences of trying to move them. One farmer who tried found himself plagued by screams in the night until he returned the stone to the circle. It is also said that it is impossible to count the stones. Those who try always arrive at a different number, no matter how many ways they count them.

The stones are believed to be a traditional meeting place of witches since ancient times, due to their mysterious power and pagan origins...

"Are you brushing up on some local history?"

Caitlyn jumped. She looked up to see Amy holding a tray containing two mugs and some ginger biscuits. She had been so engrossed in reading that she hadn't noticed the other woman return.

"Is this yours?" asked Caitlyn.

"No, that one belonged to Stan, my husband. Actually, it really belonged to James—Lord Fitzroy, I mean—who gave it to Stan so that he could get familiar with some of the local beliefs, but I don't think Stan ever read it."

Caitlyn said awkwardly, "Er... I'm sorry about your husband. I heard in the village... and on the news... It must have been a horrible shock for you..."

Amy Matthews looked at her silently for a moment, as if trying to decide what to say.

"It *was* a bit of a shock," she said at last. "But it wasn't a bad one. In fact—" she gave Caitlyn a shame-faced look, "—if you've been in the village any length of time, I'm sure you'll have picked up the local gossip. You must have heard about my husband beating me. I... I suppose it was silly of me to try and pretend earlier in the bakery."

"No, I can understand," said Caitlyn quickly. "And I'm sorry. I didn't mean to pry—"

The other woman gave a bitter laugh. "You'd be the first in this village! No one can keep their noses out of other people's business. Anyway, I don't care who knows. I'm glad Stan is dead—*glad*!" She looked at Caitlyn defiantly. "He made my life a living hell. You don't know the number of nights I've lain in bed, battered and sore, praying that Stan would have an accident while he was out in the forest... So I can't say that I'm sorry he's dead!"

Caitlyn shifted uncomfortably. The fierce emotions from the other woman surprised her and she was reminded of the gossip in the post office shop. She stole a glance at Amy Matthews. She had thought the gamekeeper's wife too weak and timid to be capable of murder but now she wasn't so sure anymore.

"Um... do the police have any theories about the murder?"

Amy shrugged, sinking down on the couch next to Caitlyn. "They've been asking a lot of questions around the village. They came and questioned me yesterday. I told them that Stan had his supper at six o'clock as usual, then cleared off to the pub and stayed there all evening, like he usually does. I was bracing myself for him to return, drunk and reeking of alcohol as usual, and probably looking for someone to punch..." She shuddered at the memory. "Then I must have fallen asleep because, the next thing, it was morning and I heard that they'd found his body..."

She looked at Caitlyn, her eyes dark. "And do you know what my first thought was? I was relieved! Relieved that there would be no more nights where Stan would come home and give me something like this." She indicated the nasty bruise on the side of her face.

"Did he do that just before he was killed?" asked Caitlyn.

Amy nodded. "The night before. We... we had a fight. He was angry that I had gone to see the Widow Mags again."

Caitlyn's ears pricked up. "The Widow Mags? You mean, at the chocolate shop?"

Amy nodded again, her eyes sparkling. "Yes! Have you tasted her chocolates? They're amazing! I wandered into the shop a few weeks ago when I was just walking around by myself, feeling down. I had a bit of money to spare and I thought—what the hell, Stan would just drink it all away anyway—so I decided to treat myself to some chocolates."

She saw Caitlyn's look of surprise and said, "Yes, I know. Everyone in the village is terrified of the Widow Mags. They say that she's a witch, that her chocolates are enchanted by dark magic. But she was kind to me. I mean, she was a bit stroppy to start with, but then it was as if she somehow knew about Stan and... and everything. I don't know how—she didn't ask and I didn't tell her—but I got the feeling that she *knew*, you know?"

Amy leaned back against the sofa cushions, her eyes growing distant as she relived the memory. "She gave me some chocolate truffles that she had been making—she said they were a special batch. Well, I don't know what she put in them but they were *incredible*. They made me feel... I don't know... braver somehow. Empowered. Like I could do anything, like I didn't have to live in fear anymore. When Stan raised his hand to me that night, I laughed in his face." She chuckled at the memory. "I don't know who was more freaked out—him or me!"

She sighed. "I went back to the chocolate shop again after that, whenever I could—whenever Stan wouldn't know about it. But I think someone must have been spying on me and told him, because he came home livid, the night before he was murdered, and told me that if I ever went back to the chocolate shop again, he'd beat me to within an inch of my life."

Amy sprang up, suddenly self-conscious. "Oh! Listen to me babbling on about myself! Sorry, I didn't mean to bore you—"

"No, not at all!" Caitlyn assured her quickly. "I'm staying at the chocolate shop myself, actually, so I guess you could say I'm a fan of the Widow Mags too." She grinned. "I'm definitely a fan of her chocolates!"

Amy laughed. "They are delicious, aren't they? So you're staying with her? Is it comfortable? I always thought the cottage looked a bit... well... run-down."

"It *is* a bit basic," Caitlyn admitted. "But I'm managing okay."

"Well, if you want somewhere else to stay..." Amy said shyly. "I'd be very happy to have you here. We have a second bedroom. It's very small but the bed's fairly comfy..."

"Oh, thank you." Caitlyn smiled. "I'm all right for now but thanks for the offer." She paused, then said, watching the other woman carefully, "By the way, I saw something strange from my bedroom window last night. It looked like someone was lighting a bonfire at the top of the hill behind the cottage—just where the stone circle would be."

Amy looked blank. "A bonfire? Really? I guess I wouldn't know—as you can see, I'm facing the other side of the village."

"I tried to ask in the village post shop this morning but I got the feeling that people didn't want to talk about it. I thought maybe it was because I was a stranger—a visitor to the village. Perhaps it's something that locals keep to themselves?"

"Well, they wouldn't tell *me*," said Amy with a bitter laugh. "They never talk to me in the village— they just talk *about* me behind my back. I don't know if it's because I'm a 'newcomer' or if it's something else."

"Have you lived here long?"

Amy shook her head. "Only a few months. We used to live in the much bigger village on the other side of the Manor. Huntingdon Manor," she added when Caitlyn looked blank.

"That sounds like something from a Regency romance," said Caitlyn with a grin.

Amy laughed. "The reality is closer than you think! Lord James Fitzroy, the owner of Huntingdon Manor estates, owns most of the land in this area— including the village of Tillyhenge."

Caitlyn stared at her. "What? He can't own the whole village! I thought that ancient feudal system had died out."

"It has in most of England but there are still pockets where it exists. Oh, not that James behaves like a feudal lord or treats us like 'serfs' or anything! He's really just a landlord, you know, and we're all his tenants. But he's very generous with the terms of our leases and he does a lot to improve the conditions in the village and our general quality of life. He really cares. And he's not afraid to get his hands dirty. During the harvest, he's out there in the fields next to the men, with his sleeves rolled up, helping out. The old Lord Fitzroy would *never* have done that! He was quite a snob but James is a really decent chap. And very handsome too," she added, grinning. "I think half the women in the village are in love with him."

"He sounds too good to be true," said Caitlyn dryly. "Don't tell me—he rides and dances and speaks six languages?"

Amy chuckled. "He does ride—he's got this beautiful Percheron stallion—but most of the time, he doesn't behave like a member of the aristocracy. He never throws his title around. I heard that he used to work as a foreign correspondent for the BBC and spent a lot of time overseas before he had to come home last year to take over the running of the estate, after the old Lord Fitzroy died. Maybe that's why he acts more like 'one of us'. It's really endeared him to the villagers, you know. They all look up to him as the unofficial head of the village and go to him for everything. In fact, when they discovered Stan's body, they went straight to the Manor to see James first, even before reporting it to the police.

"And he's been so kind to me too," Amy continued. "We don't own this house, of course—it belongs to the estate. James organised for us to move from our old accommodation to this side of the valley, so that we could have a bit more space than where we were living previously. I suppose with Stan dead now, I don't really have a right to live here anymore, but James told me that I can stay here for as long as I want, and not to worry about rent either, since I'm not working." She frowned. "But I don't want to be beholden to him. I don't like to take advantage of his generosity. I'm going to look for work as soon as I can." She sighed. "It's just hard as there's not much in the local area. My background is in secretarial work but all the offices are in the bigger villages and towns, much farther from here."

"How about looking for work online?" suggested Caitlyn. "Nowadays you can often work remotely from anywhere, as long as you have an internet connection and can use email. I'm sure you could find virtual assistant work and things like that."

Amy gave her an ironic look. "Yeah, that would be an option—if only the internet worked properly in Tillyhenge."

"What do you mean?"

"Haven't you noticed? There's some kind of internet blackout over Tillyhenge. They've tried everything but there just seems to be a problem connecting to the servers from here. It works occasionally but it's very unreliable. Mobile phones too."

Caitlyn pulled her mobile out of her pocket and glanced at it. Now that she thought about it, it was true—she had tried to ring Pomona before going to bed last night and had struggled to get through. She had assumed that it was a problem at Pomona's end; her cousin was notorious for forgetting her phone and leaving it behind somewhere or not hearing it ring if she was at a noisy party. But now as she looked at her phone again, Caitlyn noticed that there was no signal.

"Don't worry—the landlines work. The Widow Mags should have a line installed at the chocolate shop. Or you're welcome to come and use my phone here," offered Amy.

"Thanks, that's really kind. And speaking of the chocolate shop, I'd better head back now." Caitlyn rose and placed her mug on the table. "Thanks so much for the coffee."

Amy rose as well and gave her a warm smile. "It's me who should say thank you. I don't have many friends in the village and it's really nice to have someone to chat to. Come back anytime," she added shyly.

CHAPTER SEVEN

On the way back to the chocolate shop, Caitlyn thought about the strange morning she'd had. She'd come to Tillyhenge looking for answers about her past and somehow stumbled into a murder investigation! She hoped fervently that Amy Matthews wasn't involved. She liked the young woman; even though she had only met her that morning, Caitlyn had instinctively warmed to the gamekeeper's wife.

When she arrived back at the chocolate shop, Caitlyn was surprised to find that the Widow Mags was still absent. She stood in the middle of the shop area and looked around, thinking how sad and empty the room looked. It seemed wrong, when the chocolates were so delicious, that the place didn't have more business. Her gaze scanned the bare stone walls and dark wooden shelving, which gave the room such a morbid atmosphere. Aside from the counter, there was no furniture in the store, which made the central space look even more bare and empty. Then she looked at the dusty pane of the glass counter, which didn't do justice to the delicious chocolate truffles and bonbons displayed underneath.

What this place needs is a lick of paint and a bit of sprucing up, thought Caitlyn. *Maybe even a few tables and chairs arranged at one end, so people can sit and enjoy the delicious chocolate treats.* If the shop was brightened up and an inviting window display set up, she was sure more people would come in off the street. And once someone had tasted the incredible chocolates, they would be sure to tell all their friends and family, and word would spread...

Caitlyn sighed as she looked around again. It would be so wonderful to turn things around, to have the shop thriving, the room bustling with customers and people sitting down together, enjoying hot chocolate and cakes... Then she chided herself for her silly thoughts. What on earth was she thinking? It wasn't even her shop! Why did she care if it thrived or not?

She turned and marched into the back of the cottage, where she knocked on the door that led to the Widow Mags's private quarters. As she had expected, she didn't get an answer. She peeked in the kitchen and even the large pantry next to the kitchen, which was being used as a stillroom—the ceiling decorated with hanging bunches of dried leaves and flowers, and the shelves full of herbal cordials, powders, and tinctures. Nothing. No sign of the Widow Mags.

Giving up, Caitlyn wandered out the back door of the cottage and found herself in a small herb garden. Someone had lovingly staked the plants and arranged them in rows, with little labels attached to their bases. Caitlyn walked along the rows, reading the names, some familiar, some strange. *Sage, Elfwort, Poppy, Vervain, Yarrow, Mugwort, Lavender, Belladonna, Hollyhock, Basil, Mint, Foxglove...*

The path between the rows led out onto the hill and joined a trail which led up the slope, running alongside the line of trees at the edge of the woods. Caitlyn looked at the path, following its route up the hill with her eyes, and then, on an impulse, began to climb.

If the villagers weren't going to tell her the truth about the bonfire, then she would investigate for herself. And the first step was visiting the stone circle.

***

Caitlyn climbed eagerly, relishing the exercise and enjoying the fresh air. She felt happy to be doing something proactive at last and was looking forward to seeing this mythical stone circle that was so talked about. When she reached the crest of the hill, however, she forgot about the stones for a moment as she caught her breath at the magnificent view spreading out around her.

Behind her was the village, with the chocolate shop at the foot of the hill, and to her right, the forest sweeping up and over the hill, partially covering it like a dark green blanket. To the left, the rolling hills of the Cotswolds stretched away into the distance, whilst straight in front of her, the slope curved gently downwards onto a wide plain where a large manor house stood, surrounded by landscaped parks and gardens.

That must have been Huntingdon Manor, the seat of Lord Fitzroy's estate. It was an imposing eighteenth-century Georgian building, with two wings on either side of a central courtyard, beautiful classical proportions, and Palladian features. To one side was a cluster of traditional outbuildings, stables and coach house, grouped around a stable courtyard. It looked serene and majestic—the quintessential English country house.

Caitlyn turned in a slow circle, scanning the landscape again, this time stopping when she faced the forest, which clung to one side of the hill. Her eyes widened.

She saw them.

Large sarsen boulders grouped in a circle, their

misshapen forms resembling hunched warriors, frozen in time. One reared taller than the rest, easily towering over six feet, and the rest seemed to be twisted as if they were bowing towards it. Caitlyn approached the stones slowly and walked around the outside of the circle. Was it her imagination or did it seem to be suddenly quieter here, the air stiller... almost like someone holding their breath, waiting...?

A breeze stirred her hair and she heard something on the wind. Faint cries, high and eerie... almost like a baby crying and yet no human baby could sound like that...

Caitlyn shivered. Unbidden, the myth of the *banshee* and its thin, wailing cries that heralded death came to her mind, but she banished the thought and told herself that it was probably just the sound of the wind whistling through the trees. Trying to shut her ears to the faint cries, she went forwards to examine the stones more closely. She paused by one of the boulders and hesitated, then put out a hand to touch its rough, pitted surface.

Something sparked from her fingers, causing her to jump back with a yelp. Then she gave a self-deprecating laugh. Static electricity. That was all. Nothing spooky about that.

She shook her head ruefully. All those legends she'd read in that book about Tillyhenge were putting ideas into her head. These were nothing more than blocks of sandstone that had somehow been left here on the landscape. There was nothing magical about them.

Then Caitlyn saw something in the centre of the circle which made her heartbeat quicken: a shallow pit filled with black soot and the crumbling remains of burnt wood logs. So she had been right—someone *had* built a bonfire here last night. And she had a feeling that the villagers had known about it, in spite of their denials. So why had they been so secretive? What were they trying to hide?

She looked around, a feeling of unease creeping over her. Then she shook it off irritably. *Stop it!* She was letting her imagination run away with her again! The legends and myths were stories, nothing more— made up by ignorant peasants in times past or maybe even created on purpose to give the stones a more romantic image. For example, that legend about the stones being un-countable... well, that was easy enough to disprove! And she would do it now.

Caitlyn stepped into the centre of the circle and turned to face the stones, beginning to count them. *One, two, three, four, five, six, seven, eight, nine, ten, eleven, twelve, thirteen...* No, hang on... had she counted that one already?

Start again. *One, two, three, four, five, six, seven, eight, nine, ten, eleven...* No, that's not right...

Shaking her head in exasperation, Caitlyn took a deep breath and started again. *One, two, three, four, five, six, seven, eight, nine, ten, eleven, twelve, thirteen, fourteen...* She stopped again, confused. She had tried to start counting from the tallest boulder, so that she would have that as a marker for when to stop—but it seemed like the tallest boulder wasn't in the place she had thought it was when she came around the circle again.

Feeling even more uneasy now but not wanting to admit it, Caitlyn marched over to the nearest stone. She would put some kind of marker on it, she decided. That way there would be no possibility of further confusion. She was just about to stoop down and find a small rock to place on the boulder when she heard a rustling come from the forest.

She froze, her eyes riveted on the dark shadows between the trees.

There was something moving through the woods. Coming towards her. Fast.

She could hear it moving through the undergrowth, the twigs and leaves crackling under its weight. Some animal—not a horse, it was not the sound of hoofbeats—but something equally large and heavy. Then Caitlyn heard the sound of harsh panting, getting louder and louder…

A dark form shot out suddenly from the forest and rushed forwards, launching itself straight at her.

CHAPTER EIGHT

Caitlyn screamed and lurched backwards as a huge furry body slammed into her chest with the force of a battering ram. She felt a hot breath on her face as she toppled over, shrieking. She landed on the soft turf with a *thump* that knocked the breath from her body and lay for a moment, stunned.

Then she became conscious of the heavy weight on top of her. She was being pinned down by two massive paws and panic surged through her as she struggled to get free. She looked up and saw the gleam of fangs in a cavernous mouth and she screamed again with all her might.

The creature responded by leaning closer and, the next minute, Caitlyn felt something wet and slobbery on her terrified face, whilst her ears caught the sound of anxious whining.

Wait a minute... Slobbery? Anxious whining?

Slowly, Caitlyn pushed herself up on her elbows and looked at the creature before her. It was an enormous English mastiff, its saggy face and wrinkled brow furrowed in an adorable fashion as it cocked its head to one side and regarded her lovingly. Its big pink tongue was hanging out of its mouth as it panted and drooled down the front of its chest. Suddenly, Caitlyn realised that the dog had been licking her and that her face was covered in dog drool.

"*Eeuugh!* Get off me!" she gasped, trying to scramble out from beneath the mastiff.

But the huge dog simply wagged his tail and clamped a massive paw on her chest, giving her another slurp with his tongue.

"*Eeeuuuw!* Stop! That's disgusting!" cried Caitlyn, turning her face away from the big slobbery tongue. She didn't know whether to laugh or cry. Here she had thought that she was being attacked by some wild beast and instead it was simply an oversized lapdog!

She noticed that the mastiff was wearing a leather collar around its massive neck but just as she was reaching out to search for a tag, she heard a deep, male voice shouting:

"Bran! Bran, where are you?"

The next moment, a man rushed out of the woods and into the open space beside the stone circle. He flinched when he saw the mastiff on top of Caitlyn and hurried towards them.

"Bran! You stupid dog—what are you doing? I'm really sorry... Please excuse my dog. He's a big buffoon but harmless really."

He shoved the mastiff off and helped Caitlyn gently to her feet.

"I'm sorry. Did he frighten you? He's really very well trained... but... uh... suffers occasional lapses sometimes. Bran loves people and I'm afraid that he labours under the misapprehension that everyone is waiting for him to charge up and say hello."

He held a large hand out to her and gave her a lopsided smile. "My name's James. James Fitzroy."

Caitlyn stood and gawped at him. Tall, dark, and handsome didn't even come close to describing him. The man was like Mr Darcy and James Bond all rolled into one, and with the sexiest British accent to boot. He stood well over six feet tall, with broad shoulders outlined by the fine cotton of his classic polo shirt, worn over beige breeches tucked into black riding boots. Dark unruly hair swept across his forehead, in a way that Byron would have envied, and his face was defined by dark eyebrows over humorous grey eyes. His nose was slightly large but it suited him, offsetting the strong line of his jaw, which showed a hint of dark stubble. The hand he held out to her had long tapered fingers but the roughened skin on his fingertips and the bulge of muscles beneath his shirt showed that he was no mincing aristocratic fop. This was a man who was used to physical exertion and the great outdoors.

Suddenly, Caitlyn realised that she was still standing there, staring at him, open-mouthed. Hurriedly, she shut her mouth and put her hand in his.

"Uh... h-hi."

She was intensely conscious of the fact that she was covered in bits of mud and grass, with a film of dried dog drool clinging to her chin. Why-oh-why hadn't she listened to her cousin when Pomona wanted to give her a makeover? Then maybe she could have presented a more glamorous image now, instead of facing James Fitzroy in her oldest jeans and a billowing peasant-style blouse that probably piled on extra pounds—not to mention her face bare of make-up and her red hair pulled back anyhow in a messy ponytail! Caitlyn began making a desperate attempt to brush herself off and straighten her hair.

James winced as he watched her. "I'm sorry—Bran doesn't know his own strength sometimes. I hope your clothes haven't been damaged? I'd be happy to pay for any replacements."

"Um... no, it's okay... these are old things anyway," murmured Caitlyn. She rubbed her cheek, hoping to get the dog slobber off.

"Here..." said James, handing her a crisp white handkerchief.

"Thanks." Caitlyn flushed slightly as she took it.

"I'm afraid some of it has gone into your hair as well..." said James, his eyes going to her forehead.

He lifted his hand and gently brushed back a few strands of her hair.

Caitlyn caught her breath, feeling goosebumps erupt all over her skin. Hurriedly, she took a step back and babbled, "How... how come he was running loose anyway? Shouldn't he be on a leash? I thought there was a law in England where all dogs had to be on a leash in public places?"

"They do." He looked amused. "But this isn't a public place. This hill and these woods are part of the Fitzroy family estate—so this is my land."

"Oh." Caitlyn gulped. "Er... does that mean I'm trespassing?"

His lips quirked in a smile. "Yes. But I'll forgive you—on one condition."

"What's that?"

"You tell me your name. You know mine—but I haven't had the pleasure of learning yours."

Caitlyn felt herself swoon slightly. *Oh my goodness, the man even talked like someone in a Jane Austen novel!*

"My name's Caitlyn... Caitlyn Le Fey," she added after a moment's hesitation.

"Le Fey?" He frowned. "Any connection to the singer, Barbara Le Fey?"

"She was my mother... adoptive mother, actually. But I would appreciate it if you kept that to yourself," she added quickly. "I'm... er... sort of in Tillyhenge incognito and I'd like to keep it that way."

"Incognito?" He arched an eyebrow. "That sounds

intriguing. May I ask why?"

"Um... I'm... I'm searching for some answers... about my past..." Caitlyn trailed off, wondering why she had blurted that out. She hadn't revealed her real reasons for coming to Tillyhenge to anyone else, so why was she suddenly telling James Fitzroy? And yet... there was something about him that made her trust him, that made her feel like she could tell him anything...

She waited, half expecting him to ply her with more questions, but to her surprise, he merely nodded politely. Then she remembered the British and their habit of courteous reserve. James wouldn't pry further unless she volunteered more information herself. Her hand crept up to the runestone necklace, tucked out of sight beneath her blouse, but she didn't quite feel ready to show it to him. Instead, she gestured to the stone circle beside them and said:

"Do you know anything about a bonfire here?"

"A bonfire?"

"Yes, I thought I saw one from my window last night. I'm staying at the chocolate shop and my bedroom faces the hill," she explained.

He shook his head. "I didn't notice myself—but my bedroom faces the other way." He glanced into the circle, narrowing his eyes as he saw the remnants of the burnt logs in the centre. "Hmm..."

"I thought maybe it was some kind of local tradition... like a pagan ritual or something..."

"And you came here to check it out yourself?" He

raised his eyebrows.

Caitlyn flushed at the censure in his tone. "It's broad daylight and perfectly safe."

"Perhaps. But you might want to be cautious about wandering to secluded places alone." He paused, then added, "A man was murdered here recently."

"Yes, I know," said Caitlyn. "I heard on the news. He worked for you, didn't he?"

"Yes, he was my gamekeeper." James looked at her curiously. "Why did you think of pagan rituals when you saw the bonfire?"

"Oh..." Caitlyn looked down and shuffled her feet, embarrassed. "Well, I heard some people mention witchcraft in connection with the murder and I guess the idea came into my head."

He made a dismissive sound. "Some of the villagers have overactive imaginations. There was no witchcraft involved. Stan Matthews was poisoned, pure and simple. The post-mortem tests detected lethal levels of atropine in his system."

"I heard some stories about the way he was found, like his eyes turning black—"

"One of the symptoms of atropine poisoning is dilation of the pupils. Matthews's eyes were extremely dilated when we found him. It would make his previously blue eyes look black to those who only had a quick glance at him."

"Oh." Caitlyn digested this. "Do the police know where the atropine came from?"

James made a face. "That's the six-million-dollar question. If they could know the answer to that, they'd probably know the identity of the killer."

"What do you mean?"

"Well, atropine can come from a variety of sources. It's mostly used in medical applications, such as in the treatment of slow heart rates and in eye drops for ophthalmic examinations. It's also used to treat excessive sweating. In fact, it's even used as an antidote for other toxins. And of course, there are all the old folk remedies that use extracts of belladonna... Belladonna is a natural source of atropine," he explained at Caitlyn's blank look.

"Wow... you seem to know a lot about it."

James gave her a grim smile. "I've made it my business to know. The murdered man was a Fitzroy employee and I take care of my people. I want to see his killer brought to justice. The police have been very good about keeping me informed on all aspects of the case."

"So... you mean anyone with a medical connection could have got hold of the poison? Like a doctor or something?"

James nodded. "Or even anyone who is being treated for certain medical conditions. Or anyone who makes or uses herbal remedies containing belladonna. In fact, even someone who just grows belladonna in their gardens could have had access to the poison and be the killer." He gave her a sardonic look. "As you can see, that leaves the field pretty wide open."

Caitlyn was reminded uneasily of the gossip in the post office shop and the reports of belladonna growing in the Widow Mags's garden. She remembered her own stroll through the backyard of the cottage earlier and the neat rows of herbs and plants, each carefully labelled. She couldn't recall exactly but she seemed to remember seeing "*Belladonna*" amongst the names...

She cleared her throat. "But why would anyone want to kill your gamekeeper?"

"I don't know but I can make a guess. Stan Matthews liked to drink and squandered most of his income at the pub. I think he might have been tempted with an offer of extra cash and got involved in something which then backfired."

"Extra cash? You mean, he was accepting a bribe? For what?"

"For access to hunting. Gamekeepers are supposed to guard against poachers—that's one of the key roles of their job. But they are also perfectly placed to cover up any illegal hunting activity."

"You think Matthews was being paid off by poachers?"

"Yes."

Caitlyn gestured around them. "But... what would they be poaching?"

"There's a herd of deer on the estate. They live mostly in the forest and they are protected. But they would be an attractive target for poachers, especially if—" He broke off.

Caitlyn looked at him curiously. "Especially if what?"

James hesitated, then said reluctantly, "There are stories going back several generations about the White Stag and how it's been spotted in these woods."

"The White Stag?"

"It's a mythical creature," said James, looking slightly sheepish. "It's believed to be a messenger from the Otherworld and they say it appears to those who are about to set off on a new journey. It's supposed to signal a time of change and new beginnings."

"But that's just a myth, right?"

"Oh yes—I'm not suggesting that there really is a mythical White Stag in these woods," said James hastily. "But there really are red deer stags that are born white. It's very rare but they do exist and they are highly valued by poachers. There was a tragedy a few years ago when a 'white stag' on the Devon-Cornwall border was found shot and beheaded. Its carcass had been left behind but the head was gone."

"That's awful!" cried Caitlyn. "Why would they do that?"

"The head, with the antlers, is worth a lot. It could be mounted as a trophy and sold for thousands of pounds. That's why the locals had kept the white stag's existence a secret for ages, because they knew how prized he was by hunters."

"So you think people might be looking for a 'white stag' in your woods?"

"It's possible, especially if Stan Matthews had been talking it up," said James. "I've heard from my other staff that he liked bragging, especially when he got drunk. I wouldn't be surprised if he exaggerated things a bit—pretended that he had proof of a 'white stag' being found in these woods—and even accepting money to show someone where to find it."

He hesitated, then added, "The police have a few suspects on their list and one of them is a Dutch South African gentleman who arrived in the village just before Matthews's murder. His name is Hans van Driesen and he's a big game hunter. He's exactly the sort of man who would see the head of a 'white stag' as the ultimate trophy."

"Have the police questioned him?" asked Caitlyn eagerly.

"Yes, but they have no evidence to tie him to the murder... yet."

"Well, I think that—*Listen!* D'you hear that?" Caitlyn caught his arm.

"Hear what?" James frowned.

"The cries... Can't you hear them?" Caitlyn turned towards the forest. "I heard them earlier; I kept thinking it was my imagination... but now I can hear them again."

And this time, there was no question of banshees or some other fanciful explanation. No, these were obviously from an animal—an animal in terrible distress. The cries tore at Caitlyn's heart. She had to help.

She turned and rushed into the forest.

CHAPTER NINE

Something thundered next to Caitlyn and she realised that it was Bran the mastiff lumbering beside her, his big tongue hanging out and his jowls flapping up and down as he ran. Behind them, she could hear James's voice sounding annoyed and bewildered.

"Wait! Caitlyn! Where're you going—? Bran, come back!"

Caitlyn ran faster, racing around the bend of the path and coming suddenly into a clearing in the woods. There was a large pool in the centre of the clearing with edges that looked too sharply hewn to be natural. It was a disused quarry, she realised. Probably once used by the residents of the villages nearby to supply the stones for building their cottages. It had long been abandoned, however, and had filled up with rainwater, so that it was now a stagnant pool of milky green.

And in the middle, mewing and paddling frantically, was a tiny black kitten.

It was barely keeping its head above water as it tried to swim to the edge of the pool but seemed to only go around in circles instead. Caitlyn realised that she must have heard it mewing earlier, when she had first noticed the faint cries. It must have been wandering in the forest then, lost and calling for its mother, and its cries of loneliness had turned into shrill calls for help when it had fallen into the water.

"Hang on! I'm coming!" shouted Caitlyn, rushing to the edge of the pool.

"Caitlyn! Wait!" A strong masculine hand reached out and caught her wrist, yanking her back from the edge.

"There have been several drownings in this pool," said James urgently. "It's much deeper than you think and the water is treacherous—once you're in, it's very hard to get out because the sides are so steep."

"But the kitten—!" Caitlyn threw an agonised look over her shoulder just in time to see the kitten go under, then resurface, coughing and spluttering and mewing pitifully.

"We need to find a branch and extend it so that the kitten can climb—"

"There's no time!" cried Caitlyn. "By the time you

find a branch, the kitten will have drowned. *Let me go!*"

Jerking her wrist free, she turned and launched herself off the edge of the pool, landing with a huge splash in the water. Green murkiness enveloped her for a second, then she burst to the surface, shaking her hair out of her eyes. The water was cold and unpleasantly slimy, but she barely noticed as she began swimming towards the struggling kitten.

"It's all right... I'm coming..." she spluttered, pulling strongly through the water.

The kitten was failing now, its efforts to paddle getting weaker and weaker and its head sinking lower and lower into the water.

"*Me-e-ew... Me-e...*"

"Got you!"

Caitlyn caught the little black kitten by the scruff of its neck and lifted it out of the water. She propped it on her shoulders, hoping that it would have enough strength to hang on, then turned and began swimming back towards the edge of the quarry pool. She got there to find James looking down at her with a mixture of relief and exasperation.

He reached down and helped pull her out of the pool. Caitlyn wouldn't have admitted it out loud but he was right: the sides were very steep and slippery, and extended several feet above her head, making it almost impossible to find a handhold to pull herself out. She could see just how easily one could drown in that pool, just searching for a way to climb out and becoming exhausted in the deep water.

"That was an incredibly stupid thing to do!" snapped James, looking at her angrily. "You could have drowned!"

"I'm a good swimmer," said Caitlyn, stung. She staggered to her feet, dripping water everywhere. "I've swum in seas all over the world and I know what I'm doing."

"You may be a good swimmer but even the best swimmers would exhaust themselves if they had to tread water forever. If I hadn't been here, how would you have got out of the pool?"

Caitlyn opened her mouth, then shut it again. He was right. And she was annoyed that he was right.

"I would have figured out a way," she muttered.

"Do you always do this? Rush into things without thinking?"

"It's none of your business if I do!" Caitlyn retorted.

She was being rude and ungrateful, she knew, but she couldn't seem to help herself. She felt really disgusting now: the cold slimy water was dripping off her hair and running in rivulets down her face and back, her clothes were plastered to her body, and her feet squelched in her sandals.

"*Meewww...*"

"Oh, the kitten!" Caitlyn reached up and gently lifted the kitten from where it was still clinging to her shoulders. It was tiny—no more than six weeks old—and sooty black all over, except for a pair of big yellow eyes. Caitlyn could feel its little body shivering against her.

"Oh heavens, I hope it's going to be okay? It's so small! And so skinny! I wonder how long it's been in the water? What if it dies of hypothermia or water inhalation or—"

"The first thing to do is to get it warm and dry." James's calm voice cut through her panicked babbling. "I can take it back and get my stable manager to have a look. He's not a vet but he's got years of experience looking after the horses and other animals on my estate. There's no local vet in Tillyhenge—you'd have to go to one of the local towns and the delay could be fatal." He reached out large capable hands. "Will you entrust the kitten to me?"

Caitlyn looked up at him, their recent argument forgotten. She nodded and handed the kitten to him, watching as he folded it gently into the crook of his arm and tucked it close to his body. Then he looked up at her and frowned.

"Will you be all right getting back yourself? I would have liked to escort you—"

"Oh, no need to worry about me!" said Caitlyn quickly. "I'll be fine. It's only a short walk down the hill back to the chocolate shop." She hesitated. "Are you sure about the kitten? I mean, it's really not your problem and I was the one who rescued it..."

He gave her a smile, making her heart skip a beat. "If you put it like that, the kitten was found on my estate—so it *is* my business. Don't worry, I'm sure it'll be fine. I'll probably see you around—Tillyhenge is a small place—but feel free to come up to the Manor anytime if you want to check on it. I'll let my housekeeper know to expect you."

"Oh... um... thanks," Caitlyn stammered.

He gave her a nod, then turned and began to stride away through the forest.

"Come, Bran!" he called to the mastiff, who was still standing at the edge of the pool, staring quizzically into the water. The entire rescue seemed to have gone over the big dog's head and he was still sniffing the edge of the water, a baffled expression on his face.

"Bran! Come on, you dolt! The kitten's over here!" James waved impatiently.

The mastiff looked up, his wrinkled face brightening, and lumbered happily after his master.

Caitlyn watched them until they disappeared from sight, her heart full of something she couldn't define, then she began making her own way back towards the chocolate shop.

CHAPTER TEN

Caitlyn got back to *Bewitched by Chocolate* and hurried upstairs to change into dry clothes. When she returned downstairs, she was surprised to find someone in the chocolate shop: a young man in a cheap suit who was facing the old woman across the counter, holding a brochure nervously in his hands.

"...so you see, it would really be a v-very good deal for you, ma'am," he stammered. "My company, Blackmort Enterprises, would compensate you handsomely for your property. S-such an opportunity might not come again—"

"And what are you going to do with my house?" the Widow Mags demanded.

"Oh... er... well, the cottage itself isn't worth much," the young man said apologetically. "It's the land it's sitting on, really. You see, this is a fantastic location with the views and the easy access to the countryside—and the proximity to the railway. A lot of people in the cities are wanting to move out to the countryside now and the Cotswolds is one of the top destinations. And your parcel of land is quite large, which means that there would be enough space for sub-development—"

"You mean you're going to knock my cottage down and put some ugly concrete boxes in its place?"

"N-no, ma'am," said the young man. "Er... I mean... they *will* be concrete but they will follow the finest modern design principles. We have top architects working for us at Blackmort Enterprises and—"

"What about me?" the Widow Mags cut in. "What am I going to do while you're faffing around with your 'modern design principles'?"

"Oh, I'm so glad you mentioned that," the young man said eagerly. He held out the brochure. "You see, Blackmort Enterprises also manages several nursing homes and aged care communities. As I said, you will be compensated handsomely for your property. *Very* handsomely. So you will have a lump sum to invest and you won't have to worry about working anymore. You could simply enjoy your retirement in one of these luxurious properties— see?" He turned the pages of the brochure proudly. "Each unit is extremely comfortable and spacious, with its own courtyard or balcony, and you would have access to twenty-four-hour security and monitoring, as well as physiotherapists and nurses on site." He turned more pages. "And there are numerous amenities, such as bowling greens and a gym and indoor heated pool..." He glanced around the chocolate shop. "Wouldn't you rather live somewhere modern and comfortable, with someone taking care of all your needs?"

"No," the Widow Mags snapped. "I'm not so in my dotage that I need someone to wipe my bum for me."

The young man flushed. "Oh, er... th-that's not what I meant... Naturally, you still look like you're very much in your prime..." He flushed again under the Widow Mags's sardonic gaze. "Uh... I-I mean, maybe not your prime *exactly* but very w-well-preserved for someone of your advanced years... er, I mean, senior citizen... that is..."

Caitlyn felt slightly sorry for him. She didn't like salespeople in general but this young man was different. With his light brown hair and mild brown eyes, he looked a bit like a timid rabbit. He also looked very young. She wondered if this was his first job—he looked like someone who was keen to make a good impression with the boss. He'd probably volunteered to come see the Widow Mags and was realising now that he had bitten off far more than he could chew!

Stepping forwards to join them, she said, "Perhaps you should be speaking to Lord Fitzroy about this? I understand that he owns most of the land around Tillyhenge."

"He doesn't own mine," snapped the Widow Mags. "And I'm not selling it to *him* either!" She waved a hand at the young man. "Go away! I don't have time for your nonsense. I have chocolates to make."

"Um, maybe... maybe I could order something before I go?" He looked wistfully towards the hearth behind the counter, where the small black cauldron was bubbling away, the steam rising from it filled with a rich cocoa aroma. "What's that? It smells absolutely fantastic!"

"It's traditional Spanish hot chocolate," said the Widow Mags, thawing slightly at his genuine enthusiasm. "It's a secret recipe that's been in my family for generations." She pointed at the window seat at the front of the store. "Sit. I'll bring a cup over to you."

The young man meekly followed orders as the Widow Mags ladled the thick rich hot chocolate into an earthenware mug.

"Here, I'll take it for you," Caitlyn offered.

"Take this as well," muttered the Widow Mags, shoving a generous chunk of chocolate fudge cake onto a plate. "The boy looks like he needs a good meal."

Caitlyn hid a smile. She was beginning to realise that the Widow Mags's bark was a lot worse than her bite. Beneath that prickly exterior was a kind heart. She lifted the mug and plate and carried them carefully over to the young man, who was perching nervously on the window seat.

"Thanks," he said, giving her a hesitant smile and holding a hand out. "I'm David Allan, by the way. I didn't get a chance to meet you earlier when I arrived to talk to your grandmother."

"Oh, she's not my grandmother," said Caitlyn quickly.

"Really?" He looked surprised. "I thought I could see a family resemblance. You've got the same eyes…"

Caitlyn glanced back towards the old woman hunched behind the counter and was surprised to realise that the young man was right. They were much more wrinkled, of course, and drooping slightly with age, but the Widow Mags's almond-shaped hazel eyes did look very similar to her own.

"He-e-ello? Anyone home?"

A figure paused in the shop doorway, arm raised in a parody of knocking. Caitlyn looked up and her heart sank at the sight of that smirk. It was the reporter she'd met on the first day. He sauntered into the store and up to the counter.

"Widow Mags?" he asked. "I'm Rob Wiggins, freelance reporter. Do you have a moment? I'd love to ask you a few questions about the murder."

She scowled at him. "No."

He grinned, not put off. "Oh, I can see that you're busy now. But that's okay—I can wait. I'll just take a seat here, shall I?" He strolled over to the window seat and sat down next to David Allan, glancing across at the young salesman. "Mm, that looks delicious. I'll have what he's having," he said to Caitlyn.

She felt a flash of irritation at his patronising tone. She was tempted to tell him that she didn't work here and that he could go and get his own chocolate! Then she glanced across at the Widow Mags, still hunched behind the counter. With her arthritis flare up, it would be difficult for the old woman to juggle both preparing the chocolate orders and serving the customers. It would be a big help if Caitlyn lent a hand. Besides, she didn't have anything else to do anyway.

"You have to prepay for your order," she told Rob Wiggins. If they were going to have to suffer his company, they might as well get his money first!

As Wiggins fished in his wallet for the cash, he looked at Caitlyn thoughtfully. "You know, I'm still trying to figure out where I've seen you. Some B-list movie? Or cable TV show? *Dancing with the Stars*?" Suddenly he snapped his fingers. "I think I know! Barbara Le Fey. That singer who was killed in a car accident last month. I saw the pictures of her funeral. You were—"

"So what brings you to Tillyhenge?" Caitlyn cut in hastily.

He laughed and rubbed his hands. "A nice juicy murder, of course."

"Do you have any theories?" asked Caitlyn, desperate to keep him talking and distract him from the mystery of her own identity.

"Oh, I've got more than theories... I've got proof." He gave her a smug look.

"Proof of what?"

"Ah, that would be telling, wouldn't it?"

"You don't really have anything," said Caitlyn scornfully. "You're just talking big."

He looked indignant. "No, I'm not. I know who did it. I know the identity of the murderer."

"If you really knew that, why aren't you going to the police?"

"Ah, well..." He coughed importantly. "I still have to gather some key pieces of evidence."

"I thought you said you have proof."

He shifted uncomfortably. "Well, all right—I might not have the proof yet... but I know where to get it! And when I do, I'm going to make a splash." He gave her a gleeful look. "This could be my ticket to the big time. It'll be the scoop of the year! My byline will be on every front page. Maybe I'll even get my own column: *'Rob Wiggins—detective journalist extraordinaire'*!"

Caitlyn resisted the urge to roll her eyes. She'd never met anyone so cocky. On his other side, she saw David Allan politely pretending not to listen. She caught his eye, exchanging a smile with the young salesman. Then she took the money and headed back to the counter. The Widow Mags was no longer there. Instead, she was in the kitchen, standing at a gleaming black Aga stove that dominated one wall of the room and stirring a small pot filled with melted chocolate.

As Caitlyn watched, the old woman took out a bar of solid chocolate from a box and chopped it into small sections. Then she tossed them into the pot, stirring slowly and carefully. As she moved the ladle around and around, Caitlyn saw the melted chocolate change, going from an opaque, dark sludge to a smooth, glossy brown liquid.

"What are you doing?" asked Caitlyn, fascinated.

"Tempering chocolate," said the old woman.

"Tempering?"

"It's a special technique used by chocolatiers for centuries," the old woman explained, with no trace of her usual impatient manner. "The chocolate is heated and melted, then cooled by 'seeding' it—and then heated and melted again. This changes its structure. It makes the chocolate silky and glossy, and 'snap' crisply when you break it apart. Otherwise, it will look dull and waxy, and never set firm and hard."

Caitlyn paused in surprise. Now that she thought about it, the Widow Mags was right. All the chocolate in the store outside was a beautiful glossy shade, from the warm tan of milk chocolate to the deepest brown of dark chocolate, and even the creamy ivory of white chocolate too. She had always thought that chocolate just came like that—she didn't realise that it needed a special process to turn it that way.

"What are you going to do with the tempered chocolate?" she asked.

"I'm making some decorations for the cakes and truffles. Chocolate fans, lattices, and curls."

The Widow Mags removed the pot from the stove and transferred it to the huge wooden table in the centre of the room, setting it down next to a large marble slab. She scooped some melted chocolate out of the pot and poured it in the centre of the marble slab, creating a large, gleaming dark puddle. Then she took a long metal spatula and spread the puddle evenly over the marble in a long, oblong shape. She waited a moment as the chocolate cooled and hardened, then—using a sharp knife—she scored long lines along the length of the oblong. Turning the blade of the knife in the other direction, she began slicing down across the oblong with sharp flicks of her wrist.

To Caitlyn's amazement, tiny, delicate curls of chocolate seemed to spring from the edge of the blade as the Widow Mags moved across the marble. It looked almost like magic. Yet when Caitlyn reached out and touched one of the dainty swirls, it felt firm and strong. She lifted it to her lips. It melted sweetly on her tongue. She couldn't resist reaching out to pick up another curl. And another.

"Are you here to eat my chocolate or help me serve it?" grumbled the Widow Mags, but Caitlyn could see that the old woman had a twinkle in her eyes.

Then she remembered why she had come into the kitchen. "Mr Wiggins—the reporter—would like a cup of hot chocolate as well. Should I—?"

"No, I'll make it for him," said the Widow Mags. She pointed at the ladle in the pot. "Keep stirring the tempered chocolate. It mustn't cool down and harden, otherwise I'll have to start all over again."

Caitlyn moved around the table and picked up the ladle as the Widow Mags went out, leaving her alone. She obediently stirred the chocolate around and around the pot, finding the motion soothing, almost mesmerising. It was warm in the kitchen and Caitlyn felt drowsiness slide over her. She closed her eyes, inhaling the sweet, rich aroma of chocolate around her, and imagined what she would make if she was working with the chocolate herself. *More of those gorgeous curls, definitely... and maybe little rosettes and even proper roses, with delicate petals unfolding... interlocking hearts... beautiful lattices shaped like a crown... a butterfly perhaps or... a feather! Yes, lovely little curled plumes and—*

"CAITLYN?"

Caitlyn jumped, opening her eyes. She realised that the Widow Mags was back in the kitchen—she had been so engrossed in her daydream that she hadn't heard the old woman return. Then she realised that the Widow Mags was staring fixedly at the marble slab on the table. Caitlyn turned her gaze to look herself and gasped in wonder.

There, arranged across the slab, was an assortment of beautiful, delicate chocolate decorations. A pile of chocolate curls. Another one of rosettes. A beautiful single rose, its petals gently unfurling. A pair of interlocking hearts. Some delicate lattices curved around into the shape of a crown. Something that looked like a half-finished butterfly. And then a row of tiny, graceful feather plumes. All made with chocolate.

Caitlyn blinked. They all looked exactly like how she had imagined them. *How? Where had they come from?*

The Widow Mags approached the table slowly, still staring at the chocolate decorations. "Did you make these?" she said hoarsely.

Caitlyn stared. Then she shook her head. "N-no... I... of course not! How could I? I've never worked with chocolate before! All I was doing was standing here stirring the chocolate..." She turned, confused, to look at the pot at her elbow, and was surprised to see that the level of melted chocolate seemed to have gone down slightly, as if some of the chocolate had been used.

The Widow Mags gave her a strange look. "That's all? You weren't doing anything else?"

"No." Caitlyn shook her head again. "I just stirred it, exactly as you showed me, and imagined what I might make if I—" She broke off suddenly, staring back at the decorations on the marble.

No. No, it couldn't be.

She knew for sure that she hadn't moved from her position—and she didn't have the skill to create those little works of chocolate art. But the alternative was even more unbelievable: that they had somehow been created by her mind... by magic?

CHAPTER ELEVEN

A commotion in the shop made Caitlyn and the Widow Mags both whirl around and hurry back. Caitlyn was surprised to see that it was much fuller than when she had left. Several tourists seem to have drifted in, as well as a few villagers who stood fearfully in the front doorway, peering inside.

The loud commotion was coming from a group of women who were milling around the centre of the store, amongst them a lady Caitlyn recognised from the bakery that morning. *Angela.* The tall blonde woman who had made the malicious comments about Amy Matthews. Now she stood at the front of the group, obviously their unofficial leader.

"So... this is what the inside of the chocolate shop looks like." She wrinkled her nose as she looked around. "What a dump." She laughed contemptuously. "I can't believe everyone has been too scared to come in here for years and it's nothing but a dingy little hole."

"What do you want?" growled the Widow Mags.

"Me? Oh, just to have a browse around. Surely I'm allowed to do that?" She sauntered up to the counter and eyed the truffles on display beneath the glass pane. She gave the Widow Mags a patronising smile. "Perhaps I should buy some chocolates? The non-poisonous ones, of course." She laughed at her own joke and her friends laughed along with her.

"They're not for sale to you," the Widow Mags snapped.

Angela raised her eyebrows "Surely you're not going to turn my money away? I heard that you were really struggling... I'm sure you could use some cash." She laughed again and pulled a wad of notes out of her purse, waving them under the old woman's nose.

When the Widow Mags remained stony-faced and unresponsive, Angela's lips tightened and she thrust the money back into her bag. Then she picked up a beautiful filigree chocolate sculpture from the top of the counter.

"Wow... It must have taken you a long time to make this..." The chocolate sculpture slipped from her fingers and crashed to the floor, smashing into several pieces.

Angela covered her mouth in mock dismay. "Oops! How careless of me."

Caitlyn felt a surge of anger. That sculpture had been a beautiful piece of artwork, never mind a delicious creation of expensive chocolate. It was unforgivable to smash it on the floor like that. It was completely wasted now.

Angela turned from the counter, flinging out her arm as she did so and—accidentally on purpose— knocked another chocolate sculpture off the counter and onto the floor. More pieces of broken chocolate scattered across the wooden floorboards.

"Oh dear. I'm just so clumsy today. I don't know what's come over me." Angela smirked.

The other women laughed and one of them, emboldened by Angela's actions, reached out to a nearby shelf and knocked some chocolate bars off, then stepped on them, grinding them with her heel.

"Oh! How careless of me too! I must look where I'm stepping more." She giggled.

"Stop it," said Caitlyn, furious.

She took a step forwards. She noticed that David Allan had risen in consternation from his seat by the window, whilst next to him, Rob Wiggins was maliciously enjoying the show. The tourists hovered, uncertain, and, in the doorway, the other villagers watched with anticipation.

"Um, excuse me... You shouldn't... you really shouldn't do that..." David Allan said weakly.

Angela laughed again, then turned back to the counter where the last chocolate sculpture stood, alone and vulnerable. She lifted a languid hand and reached towards it.

"Take your hands off my chocolate." The Widow Mags's voice rang across the room, hard and cold.

Angela hesitated, then tossed her head and said with a show of bravado, "Or you'll what? Turn me into a toad?" She leaned towards the old woman suddenly, narrowing her eyes and saying in a vicious voice, "We all know you murdered that gamekeeper, you old witch! And these chocolates of yours—they're bewitched by dark magic! They're dangerous! The village has put up with you for far too long. There's no place for witchcraft here. It's time you left and took your vile chocolates with you!"

The Widow Mags said nothing.

Angela laughed again, an ugly jeering sound, then turned and picked up the last chocolate sculpture. She tossed it carelessly over her shoulder and Caitlyn flinched as it hit the floor and smashed into a dozen pieces.

Angela smiled, then made a great show of dusting her hands. There were smears on her fingers, where the chocolate had melted slightly. She rubbed these away. Then she rubbed them again. And again.

Caitlyn saw that instead of disappearing as Angela rubbed her hands together, the chocolate smears seemed to be multiplying, springing up across her skin and gradually up her arms.

"What's... what's happening to me?" gasped Angela, staring at her arms.

The smears were rising up now, forming strange

blobs and shapes...

Warts.

There were chocolate warts starting to grow all over Angela's arms, neck, and face.

"Eeeeek! Angela, your nose! Your nose!" her friend shrieked, pointing wildly.

Angela groped at her nose, feeling an enormous wart protrude from the tip.

"AAAAAGGHH!" she screamed. She clamped both hands to her face, covering her nose, and turned to the Widow Mags in fury.

"What have you done to me?" she demanded. "Undo it!"

The Widow Mags looked at her calmly. "What do you mean? If you handle chocolate, it's likely to melt and smear on your skin. Everyone knows that."

The woman next to Angela gave a cry and touched her neck. Caitlyn could see a chocolate wart beginning to grow on her throat too.

"No!" she cried, scrubbing at her neck frantically. "No! No! No! Noooo!"

The other women in the group started clutching parts of their bodies too, gasping and shrieking.

"You! You evil witch—you hexed us!" cried Angela, her voice weirdly muffled as she still had both hands clamped over her nose. "I'm going to report you to the police! I'm going to go to the Inspector right now and show him these warts. He'll come and arrest you for witchcraft!"

Turning, she stormed out of the shop, followed by

her still-shrieking friends. Silence descended on the store. The tourists were staring wide-eyed; the villagers—the ones who hadn't run off with Angela—looked terrified but fascinated.

"What are you all staring at?" snapped the Widow Mags.

Quickly, everyone looked away. Muttering under their breaths, they all scrambled to leave. Five minutes later, Caitlyn sighed as she surveyed the empty shop, the window seat abandoned, the hot chocolate half drunk. Even David Allan had mumbled an excuse and hurriedly left. It had all been going so well, the chocolate shop finally getting some customers at last...

Still, she couldn't say that she was completely sorry. There had been something wonderfully satisfying about seeing Angela and her friends get their comeuppance. Caitlyn didn't want to think too much about *how* they had got their comeuppance. Somehow, the "hoax" explanation didn't really work anymore. And yet, in spite of what had also happened back in the kitchen—with those chocolate decorations just appearing like that—Caitlyn couldn't bring herself to say the "m" word.

"Mother!" Bertha stormed suddenly through the shop's front door, her frizzy red hair flying loose, her kaftan trailing behind her. "Mother, what have you been doing? Angela Skinner is running around the village green with a group of her friends, ranting and raving about you putting a hex on her and giving her warts. Is it true?"

The Widow Mags didn't even pretend to look sorry. In fact, her eyes gleamed and she looked like a mischievous child who had done something naughty—and enjoyed it.

"Mother, how could you have done that?" wailed Bertha. "You know how hard it is already to be accepted in this village. We need to keep a low profile! People don't understand our gifts and it's dangerous if we're too open about them! Plus, you're setting a bad example for Evie. How can I tell her not to—"

"Oh, don't fuss," said the Widow Mags irritably. "It's only chocolate. Angela won't be permanently harmed." She paused, then added under her breath, "More's the pity."

Bertha sighed and said in exasperation, "Mother, can't you at least *try* to blend in a bit more?"

"Blend in?" The Widow Mags gave a cackling laugh, which startled Caitlyn. The old woman really did sound like the stereotypical witch in children's books and movies.

"We're never going to *blend in*! When are you going to realise that? Look how many years we've tried to keep our heads down and not attract attention. How long we've been suffering abuse and insults from women like Angela. People avoiding us in the street, not serving us in the shops, giving us dirty looks and talking behind our backs... We're 'different' and they'll never let us forget it. No matter how much you try to befriend them or pass yourself off as some common herbalist, it's never going to work. Besides..." The old woman gave a fierce nod. "I am what I am. I make no apologies for that."

Before Bertha could answer, there was a commotion at the front door again and, the next moment, Angela stormed back in, followed by her friends, two men in police uniforms, and an older man in a sombre grey suit. He didn't have a badge visible but there was no doubting that he was a CID detective. Caitlyn felt a prickle of unease.

"There! That's her! That's the witch!" Angela's voice was still strangely muffled because she was keeping both hands clamped over her nose. The skin on her arms and hands were clear now, the chocolate warts gone.

The detective inspector looked slightly weary as he came forwards and said, in a slow, patient voice, "Miss Skinner, as I have told you already, the police do not deal with incidences of... *ahem*... paranormal activity and the occult. So unless a crime has been committed here—"

"She hexed me! That's a crime, isn't it?"

"I'm afraid a... er... hex isn't included on the list of criminal offences under the Crown Prosecution Service."

"Well, she... she caused me harm, then! Bodily harm!" said Angela wildly. "You can arrest her for that!"

The inspector gave her a sceptical look. "Do you have proof of that?"

"Yes. It's here... on my nose." Angela said, still not taking her hands away.

"I will need to see it."

Angela hesitated, then flushing with humiliation, she removed her hands from her face. Caitlyn leaned forwards. She could see what looked like a large brown blob on the end of the woman's upturned nose.

The inspector looked slightly confused. "What am I supposed to be seeing?"

"This!" cried Angela, going slightly cross-eyed as she looked down at her own nose and pointed to the brown blob. "See? It's a hideous wart! She gave it to me—that bloody old witch!"

The inspector leaned forwards. "All I see is a bit of chocolate stuck to the end of your nose, ma'am."

"Huh?" Angela dabbed at the brown blob and it came off—a big, melted glob of chocolate, smearing across her fingers. Her eyes widened in disbelief and outrage. "Aaah! She changed it! She changed it back!"

"Miss Skinner," said the inspector, his voice no longer patient. "I do not find your joke amusing. It is a serious offence to waste police time—"

"It *was* a wart! I'm telling you, it was! It was!" Angela was almost jumping up and down with frustration.

The inspector was getting irritable now. "If you persist in these ridiculous accusations, I will be obliged to arrest you for making a false report, and wasting police time and resources."

"Aaaarrrggghh!" Shrieking in fury and outrage, Angela turned and stormed back out of the store, followed by her friends.

Caitlyn couldn't help but smile. It was good to see the horrible woman thwarted. And she felt a sense of relief that the police hadn't arrested the Widow Mags. But that relief was short-lived when she saw that instead of leaving, the inspector turned towards the counter and addressed the old woman.

"As it happens, I was on my way here to see you, ma'am. My name is Detective Inspector Walsh. Is there a room where we may speak in private?"

"Why?" asked the Widow Mags suspiciously.

The inspector gave her a hard look. "Because I am conducting an investigation into the murder of Stan Matthews and I need to ask you some questions."

CHAPTER TWELVE

Bertha clutched the Widow Mags's arm. "Mother, you don't have to answer any questions! The police can't interview you if you want to get legal advice first. I know a lady; she's a lawyer and she specialises in helping people with 'alternative' lifestyles, and she's happy to do pro bono—"

"A lawyer? Why would I want to speak to a lawyer?" said the Widow Mags. She waved a hand at the inspector. "Go ahead. Ask what you like. I have nothing to hide. But make it quick," she added, scowling at him. "I'm busy and I haven't got all day."

The inspector looked slightly nonplussed at being reprimanded like a small boy. He cleared his throat in an official manner and said:

"I believe that Mrs Matthews—the dead man's wife—is one of your customers?"

The Widow Mags's bottom lip jutted out. "So what if she is?"

"Eyewitnesses report that she was seen here in the shop with you the day before Stan Matthews was murdered. Can I ask what she purchased from you?"

"Chocolate, what else?" said the Widow Mags impatiently.

"What kind of chocolate?" the inspector persisted.

"All sorts. How do you expect me to remember? I have so many kinds." The old woman gestured around the shop.

The inspector's gaze followed her gesture. "Yes, and I hope you will have no objection to us taking a sample of each—just for comparison purposes, you understand."

"What do you mean?"

"The post-mortem report on Stan Matthews indicates that he was poisoned. Traces of chocolate were found on his fingers, and the remains of chocolate in his stomach."

"What are you trying to say?" demanded the Widow Mags. "Are you suggesting that it was my chocolates that poisoned him?"

"We just like to cover all lines of enquiry," said the inspector.

"Take whatever you want. I said I have nothing to hide."

Inspector Walsh motioned to one of the uniformed men and they watched as the young constable moved behind the counter and began taking samples of the truffles on display.

"I believe that you grow herbs as well, is that right, ma'am?" the inspector continued.

The Widow Mags gave him a surly look. "So? Lots of people grow herbs."

"Perhaps... but most don't grow certain dangerous plants such as belladonna. I understand you have several specimens in your garden. I find it interesting; why would someone who runs a chocolate shop need to grow such deadly herbs?"

"There's nothing wrong with growing belladonna if it is handled with care," said the Widow Mags huffily. "It's the fools who mess 'round without the knowledge of how to use it, who get into trouble."

"And I presume you have that knowledge?" the inspector said, looking at her intently. "In particular, using belladonna as a poison?"

"Why would I want to use it as a poison?"

"Well, I can imagine several instances. For example, if someone came to you for help... such as Mrs Matthews?" The inspector leaned forwards. "It was well known around the village that her husband beat her. It would have been understandable if she'd wanted to... get rid of him, so to speak. Perhaps you sympathised with that. Perhaps you helped her."

The Widow Mags gave him a belligerent look. "Amy Matthews didn't come to me for help to get rid of her husband... but I wouldn't have blamed her if she had. Stan Matthews was nothing but a drunk and a vicious bully. I think he got what he deserved. Good riddance!"

Bertha groaned and hid her face in her hands. "Mother..."

The Widow Mags waved dismissively at the inspector. "Now, unless you've got more stupid questions to ask me, I'd thank you to leave. I've got a shop to clean up and your constables aren't helping, stepping everywhere with their size ten feet!"

The inspector looked taken aback. He glanced around, trying to come up with a dignified response. The young constable, who had been gathering samples, had just returned from the rear of the cottage, a plastic bag with green clippings in his hand.

He nodded at the inspector. "That's everything, guv."

Inspector Walsh turned back to the Widow Mags and cleared his throat. "*Ahem...* er... yes, that will be all for now, but we may have some more questions for you later. I advise you not to leave Tillyhenge without informing the police."

The Widow Mags snorted. "Leave? Where do you think I'd be off to? A world cruise?"

The inspector turned slightly red, cleared his throat again, and left the shop with a look of relief on his face, the two police constables hurrying after him. There was a reproachful silence in the shop after they left. Bertha looked like she was fuming and about to explode at any moment. Feeling slightly embarrassed, Caitlyn grabbed a broom and hurriedly began sweeping up the scattered chocolate pieces.

As she swept, she could hear the Widow Mags and Bertha bickering in low, angry voices—then after a while, she realised that they were no longer talking about the police visit and the murder. No, they were talking about *her*. She could see them throwing speculative glances at her as they argued and she saw Bertha go into the kitchen, then return, a stunned look on her face. She must have seen the chocolate decorations—those crazy, beautiful, dainty works of chocolate art that seemed to have materialised out of thin air.

Then she paused in her sweeping. This was stupid. Why was she hesitating? She'd been in Tillyhenge over a day now and still hadn't started asking the questions she really came here for. They were obviously talking about her anyway. Now was as good a time as any.

Taking a deep breath, Caitlyn put her broom down and walked over to the counter where the two women were still talking. She reached under her shirt and pulled out the runestone attached to the ribbon around her neck.

"Um... Can you help me with something? Do you... Have you seen symbols similar to these anywhere around Tillyhenge? Do you know what they might mean?"

They froze and stared at the runestone she was holding up to show them.

"Where did you get that, girl?" the Widow Mags

asked hoarsely.

Caitlyn was surprised by their strong reactions. "It was... um... sort of given to me. I've had it since I was a baby."

"Who gave it to you?"

"I don't know." Caitlyn hesitated, then said in a rush, "I think it might have been my mother. But I don't know her. I... I only found out recently that I was adopted and that I was found as a baby by the side of the road, somewhere here in the Cotswolds. There was no ID on me. The only thing I had was this stone, on a ribbon, around my neck." When they didn't speak, she hurried on: "I... I thought it might help me find my mother—and my real family. I showed this runestone to a professor in Oxford and he told me that he thought it might be connected to the stone circle here at Tillyhenge. That's why I'm here."

The Widow Mags reached out slowly and picked up the runestone, brushing her thumb over the carved surface, whilst Bertha watched, her eyes wide. There was a strange expression on both their faces.

Caitlyn said urgently, "You know something about this, don't you? I can see it in your eyes. You recognise the stone! Where is it from? What do the symbols mean?"

The Widow Mags dropped the runestone suddenly, as if it was burning hot, and turned sharply away. "I don't know what you're talking about, girl."

"What?" Caitlyn looked at her, confused and taken aback for a moment. Then she grabbed the old woman's arm. "No, no… you *do* know something! You must tell me!"

The old woman shook her hand off. "I think you've been told a lot of nonsense. People are always making up stories about the stone circle. There's probably no connection to Tillyhenge at all—"

"Mother…" said Bertha in an agonised voice. "Mother, we can't just—"

"*Quiet!*" the Widow Mags hissed. She pushed past Caitlyn and walked over to grab the broom. Then she turned her back on them and began sweeping. It was obvious that the conversation was over.

Caitlyn turned to Bertha but the other woman avoided her eyes. She mumbled something about needing to get back to *Herbal Enchantments* and hurriedly left the chocolate shop.

Caitlyn blew out a sigh of frustration. What was going on? Why wouldn't they talk to her?

***

The pub was heaving when Caitlyn arrived there for dinner that evening. With no other restaurant in the village, it looked like it was the only place where the locals could meet up and socialise. Several people were grouped around the bar counter, nursing pints of beer, whilst others huddled around the room in wooden booths and sets of armchairs, and at various wooden tables scattered around the place.

Many people looked up and eyed Caitlyn curiously as she entered, amongst them a big man standing at the bar, a pint of ale in his hand. He had a tanned, weather-beaten face—obviously someone who normally lived in a sunny climate—which really stood out amongst the pale English villagers, and a large belly which strained against the buttons of his checked shirt. His eyes were blue, small, and shrewd, and his mouth was pursed thoughtfully beneath a greying moustache. Despite his casual clothes, he exuded an air of wealth and authority, like a man who was used to getting what he wanted and rich enough to make it happen.

Caitlyn realised that he was standing next to Rob Wiggins, the reporter, who seemed to be trying to ask him some questions, while busily scribbling on a notepad. But when he saw her, the big man made a dismissive gesture to the reporter and left the bar, coming towards her.

"You must be the young lady who arrived yesterday that I've heard so much about. I'd been hoping we might meet." He gave her a wink. "Any chance I could buy you a drink? We strangers in the village have to stick together, you know."

He had distinctive clipped accent—a South African accent—and Caitlyn realised that this must have been Hans van Driesen, the big game hunter that James Fitzroy had mentioned. She also remembered that this man was a suspect in the murder investigation and her interest quickened.

"My name is van Driesen. Hans van Driesen," he said with a smile, offering her a large hand.

She shook it and introduced herself. "What brings you to this part of England, Mr van Driesen?" she asked casually.

"I came to kill something... but don't worry, not a man," he added, bursting out laughing at the look on her face. "Oh, come, Miss Le Fey. You want to know my connection to the murder, don't you? I know everyone in the village is talking about me. They saw the police come to interview me yesterday. They think I killed that gamekeeper."

He was trying to shock her. Caitlyn felt slightly annoyed. She kept her voice deliberately cool as she asked, "And do they have good reason to suspect you?"

"Maybe." He eyed her with amusement. "I had some dealings with Stan Matthews."

"Oh? What sort of dealings?"

He leaned forwards and grinned at her. "Have dinner with me and I'll tell you."

Caitlyn hesitated. She didn't like his smug manner and the way he was manipulating her into having dinner with him. On the other hand, her interest *was* piqued in spite of herself. And besides, she did have to eat dinner anyway—why eat alone? She might as well eat with him and hear what he had to say.

"All right." She nodded at him. "You're on."

CHAPTER THIRTEEN

Caitlyn was conscious of many eyes following her as they gave their orders at the bar and then sat down together at a table. She wondered what the gossips were going to say about them the next day. The food arrived fairly quickly and, as they started eating, Caitlyn waited for van Driesen to broach the subject of the murder. But he seemed content to spend the evening making small talk and flirting with her. Finally, as they were lingering over dessert, Caitlyn decided that she had had enough. She had only agreed to eat with him for the chance of getting information and she wasn't going to let him wriggle out of that.

"So you said you had dealings with Stan Matthews," she said without preamble. "Is that what the police were interested in when they questioned you?"

He leaned back and laughed. "My dear young lady, I'm sure you've heard from local gossip that I enjoy hunting. Especially big game. Back in my homeland of South Africa, my home is full of the mounted heads of lions, Cape buffalo, elephants, and rhinos."

"The Cotswolds doesn't seem like the kind of place that would be of much interest to a big game hunter," commented Caitlyn.

He gave her a condescending smile. "Ah, but you see—there *is* something here that is very valuable to a hunter like me. A magnificent creature, rarely seen, even more rarely caught."

"You're talking about the White Stag," Caitlyn guessed.

The South African inclined his head in approval. "Bravo. You're a smart girl. Yes, I came to Tillyhenge because I had heard rumours of the White Stag being spotted in the forest nearby."

Caitlyn pulled back in disgust. "I can't believe you're actually admitting to wanting to hunt such a rare creature!"

He raised his eyebrows. "There is no law against hunting deer in Britain during the season. Whatever their colour."

"But... but it's such a senseless, cruel act! What's the point? To kill such a magnificent creature just to stuff its head and put it on your wall?"

He shrugged. "If you are not a hunter, you cannot

understand. You think it is all about the guns and the blood, but really, I am simply a collector of fine specimens of nature."

Caitlyn had to resist the temptation to argue. It was no use debating the morality of hunting for sport with Hans van Driesen, she reminded herself. It was a waste of time. The man would never change his mind and she would never be able to agree with his point of view. Instead, she said:

"So you paid Stan Matthews to show you where the White Stag was?"

He gave her a lazy smile. "Oh no, not at all. I got talking to Mr Matthews after I arrived and he informed me that the deer season ended on the 30th of April. It's illegal to shoot deer during the summer." He shrugged his big shoulders. "I had to swallow my disappointment but, like any sporting huntsman, I conceded defeat."

"So how come you're still here?"

He smiled innocently. "I enjoy the village, the English countryside. I decided to stay a bit longer. Why not? Many tourists come to the Cotswolds for a vacation—why not me too?"

"Still, I—" Caitlyn broke off, distracted, as someone walked past and banged into her chair.

She looked up to see Rob Wiggins standing next to them. He was sweating profusely and eyeing the glass of water next to her plate.

"Are you drinking your water?" He asked. "If not, can I have it? My mouth is parched."

"Oh... sure, help yourself..." said Caitlyn in surprise, watching as the young reporter grabbed her glass and gulped down the water. He looked slightly feverish, his eyes glazed and unfocused. She wondered if he might be coming down with the flu or something.

"Are you okay?" she asked him.

"I'm all right," he said, slurring his words. "Just got to get out and get some fresh air..."

He stumbled past her and lurched his way towards the pub entrance. Caitlyn turned around to watch him over her shoulder.

Hans van Driesen chuckled. "Looks like young Wiggins can't hold his drink."

Caitlyn turned back, glancing absently around the pub. It was even busier now and as the crowd shifted and parted, she suddenly spied a blonde head by the bar, close to where Rob Wiggins had been standing earlier. It was Amy Matthews, she realised in surprise. She hadn't noticed the gamekeeper's wife when she had first come in. Before she could decide if she wanted to call Amy over to join them, the front door opened again.

Caitlyn glanced over, then did a double take. James Fitzroy had just stepped into the pub, stooping slightly to fit his tall frame under the low-beamed ceilings. His eyes scanned the room and paused at her table, his mouth tightening for a moment as he saw her dinner companion, then he turned and looked away.

As Caitlyn watched from the corner of her eye, he moved slowly through the crowd, smiling and nodding and greeting various villagers. Then his eyes lit up and he made his way over to Amy Matthews. He made a gesture, obviously offering to buy her a drink. Amy smiled shyly and then, as James said something else, tossed her head back and laughed. Caitlyn was struck suddenly by how pretty the gamekeeper's wife looked, with the soft pub lighting glowing on her honey blonde hair, and her blue eyes alive with laughter. Even the ugly bruise on the side of her face couldn't mar her English-rose looks.

Caitlyn glanced at James. He was laughing too, his grey eyes crinkled at the corners and his firm mouth curved with humour. They were about the same age, she thought—James was probably in his early thirties and Amy a few years younger—and they made a handsome couple, standing there together: she so fair and him so dark.

"More coffee?"

"Hmm?" Caitlyn pulled her distracted gaze back to Hans van Driesen opposite her. "Oh, um... no thanks."

"In that case, if you'll excuse me, I am going to take a visit to the men's room."

Van Driesen got up and left her alone at the table. He had barely disappeared down the corridor at the back of the pub when a deep, male voice spoke next to her.

"I'm surprised to see you having dinner with that

man."

Caitlyn turned in surprise to see James Fitzroy towering over her. His dark brows were drawn down over his eyes, which were no longer laughing.

"What do you mean?" she asked.

"I told you van Driesen is a suspect in the murder case," he said curtly. "Do you really think it's wise to be socialising with him?"

"I think you're overreacting. I asked him about the murder—he was very upfront about it all. He admitted that he had come to Tillyhenge looking for the White Stag but when he found out that the hunting season was over, he abandoned his original plans."

James gave a scornful laugh. "And you believe him? That's the same story he spun for the police. There is no way a seasoned hunter like van Driesen wouldn't have known the dates of the English hunting season before he left South Africa. And there is no way he would just accept defeat and give up on a trophy like the White Stag just because of a silly bureaucratic detail like that. Surely you can't be that naïve?"

Caitlyn flushed. "Well... even if that's true, it still doesn't make him a murderer," she blustered.

"He was the one who found Stan Matthews's body," said James. "Did he tell you that?"

"No," Caitlyn admitted.

"That alone puts him high on the list of suspects. He was also one of the last men to be seen with

Matthews, here at the pub on the night of the murder. Did he happen to mention *that*?"

Reluctantly, Caitlyn shook her head again. Then she said with a hint of defiance, "If there was any real evidence against him, surely the police would have arrested him already?"

"The police are still gathering evidence," said James impatiently. "That doesn't mean that, in the meantime, you do stupid things like eat and drink with a man who could be using poison to kill people."

"I know what I'm doing," said Caitlyn, bristling at his words.

"Like the way you did earlier today when you jumped in the quarry pond?" he asked. "There won't always be someone like me there to help you out of trouble."

"I don't need someone like you to help me out of trouble," snapped Caitlyn, springing up from her chair. "I can manage perfectly fine by myself!"

Grabbing her handbag, she turned and saw van Driesen returning to the table, a look of surprise on his face. She thanked him curtly for the meal, then stormed out of the pub without looking at James Fitzroy again.

Outside, the evening air felt cool on her flushed cheeks and she took a few deep breaths to calm herself before she began walking back to the chocolate shop. Unlike the pub, the rest of the village seemed eerily empty, the streets dark and silent. Caitlyn found that the darkness disorientated her, making landmarks she had known well in the daytime look strange and unfamiliar.

She paused uncertainly as the street forked into two, trying to remember if she should take the left or the right lane. After a moment, she made a decision and hurried down the winding left lane, her steps echoing on the cobbled stones. Then she slowed, frowning. Were those her steps echoing or were they... footsteps behind her? She glanced over her shoulder but it was hard to see in the darkened lane.

Caitlyn paused, straining her ears to listen.

Silence.

Had she imagined the footsteps or had the other person stopped too? That would mean they didn't want her to know they were following her... which would mean that they had a sinister motive...

Caitlyn swallowed uneasily and began walking again, quickening her pace. A moment later, she heard it distinctively: the sound of footsteps hurrying in her wake. Not an echo. No, this was someone following her.

Caitlyn threw another nervous glance over her shoulder. Someone was stalking her—who was it? And why?

CHAPTER FOURTEEN

Caitlyn began walking even faster. Then she realised something with a sickening lurch of her heart. She had taken the wrong turn at the last fork; this was the wrong lane. To get to the chocolate shop, she would have to turn back and retrace her steps—which meant that she would meet her stalker.

For a moment, the thought filled her with dread—then a wave of anger wiped out everything else. She wasn't going to let someone reduce her to skulking in the dark, like some frightened rabbit!

The footsteps behind her were coming nearer and nearer now. Caitlyn slowed her own steps and listened, waiting... Then, without warning, she jerked around and faced her stalker. Someone crashed into her. She swung wildly with a fist and felt it connect with something hard and rubbery.

"Oww!" Caitlyn shook her hand. She had never tried to punch anyone before and didn't realise that it would hurt.

"Ouch! Young lady, that was uncalled for!"

Caitlyn stared in disbelief. It was the old man she had met back in Meadowford-on-Smythe—the one who had been babbling about vampires. He had some weird name... Viktor. That was it: Viktor Dracul.

He was standing in front of her now, rubbing his nose and looking at her grumpily. Caitlyn wondered how on earth he had ended up in Tillyhenge. They were miles away from Meadowford—even if he had wandered out of his nursing home again, surely he couldn't have walked this far? But then how had he got here? With a seniors' group outing? She hadn't seen any coaches with senior citizens arriving in the village earlier today, and besides, wasn't it just too much of a coincidence?

"Viktor? How did you get here?"

He looked surprised. "I am a vampire. I can travel long distances with ease."

Caitlyn groaned. Not this vampire rubbish again.

"Look, you've got to stop this silly pretence," she said impatiently. "You're not a vampire, okay? Vampires don't exist. If you're lost or homeless or something—"

"Homeless? Me?" The old man bristled with offended dignity.

Caitlyn looked at him again more carefully. She

realised that while he might have looked old and decrepit, he was scrupulously clean and well groomed, his few strands of grey hair carefully combed over his balding head. His black suit and white shirt might have been very dated but they were made of good quality fabric and beautifully pressed. In fact, if she didn't know better, she would have thought that he was some ancient aristocrat who had somehow travelled through time and ended up in the twenty-first century.

She pulled herself up short. What ridiculous ideas was she thinking? The man was simply a delusional octogenarian who had somehow escaped from a nursing home.

"Viktor," she said gently, reminding herself that he was old and probably confused. "If you need help finding your way back home, I'd be happy to—"

"Help finding my way back home?" He looked baffled. "What on earth are you talking about? I am your uncle, Caitlyn—well, not your blood uncle, of course, since I am a vampire—and I have sworn to watch over you. I am keeping my promise and giving you my protection."

"Er, thanks… but I don't need your protection," said Caitlyn, thinking now that the old guy was seriously nuts.

"Oh, but you do! You do not realise how vulnerable you are—"

"I don't need your protection," said Caitlyn again through gritted teeth, starting to lose patience. "I just need you to stop following me and go home, okay?"

"But then who is going to protect you?"

"I don't need anyone to protect me!" Caitlyn roared. His words touched a nerve after James Fitzroy's rebukes at the pub. "I can take care of myself and I don't need you! Just go away! *Go away!*"

The old man stared at her, his sunken mouth opening and closing, then he turned and shuffled away.

Caitlyn heaved a sigh of exasperation. *Good riddance*, she thought. Whirling around, she began to make her way back to the fork in the lane where she had gone wrong. But she had barely gone a few feet when her steps faltered. She remembered the expression on the old man's face; the way he had shuffled away, with his head hanging and his shoulders drooping. She winced. She had hurt his feelings. Feeling bad now, she turned back.

"Viktor... look, I'm sorry. I didn't mean to shout at you. I just... Viktor?" She peered around in confusion. There was no sign of the old man anywhere. Caitlyn frowned. The empty lane stretched in front of her. Where had he gone? There was a movement above and Caitlyn glanced upwards, but it was nothing—only a bat flying off into the night.

She frowned again. Perhaps Viktor had ducked into a doorway? Gone into one of the cottages lining this street? Then she gave a mental shrug. There was no point standing here in the dark, wondering. It seemed that here was another mystery to add to those already piling up around her.

Sighing, Caitlyn turned again and began retracing her steps, heading back towards the chocolate shop.

***

"Caitlyn? Oh thank God I finally got through to you!"

"Pomona? What's wrong?" asked Caitlyn, yawning and rubbing her eyes.

The chirpy sound of her cell phone ringing had roused her from the depths of sleep and she had stumbled out of bed and groped around the room until she'd found where she had left the phone last night. The last thing she had expected to hear when she answered it, though, was her cousin's voice shrill with relief.

"*What's wrong?*" Pomona burst out. "Do you realise how frantic I've been? You promised to call me when you got to Tillyhenge, remember? So when I didn't hear from you, I tried to call you myself but I couldn't get through. I've been, like, trying all day yesterday. I was worried sick about you!"

Caitlyn winced. "The phone reception is a bit patchy here. Sorry, I did try to call you the first night I arrived but there was no signal so I thought I'd try again the next day. But then things just started happening yesterday and the day sort of flew by in a blur. I... I guess I got side-tracked and forgot."

"What do you mean 'things just started

happening'?" asked Pomona suspiciously. "What's going on over there?"

"Just... a few strange things that are hard to explain..."

"Like what? Tell me everything!" Pomona insisted.

So Caitlyn did, recounting everything that had happened to her since she had arrived in Tillyhenge—everything except her encounters with James Fitzroy, that is. She didn't know why—she normally told Pomona everything—but she didn't want to talk about James. She also decided not to mention her encounters with that strange old man, Viktor. Somehow, it seemed so bizarre that she felt embarrassed even telling Pomona about them.

"So I don't get it," said Pomona. "It sounds like you've been sucked into this murder investigation and they've got, like, a bunch of suspects: it might be the dead man's battered wife because she wanted to stop him beating her... it might be the South African hunter dude because he was, like, doing some kind of poaching deal that went wrong... or it might be this old woman that you're staying with, this Widow Mags who owns the chocolate shop—"

"I don't think it's her," said Caitlyn quickly.

"Okay, so what's the weird stuff that's been happening?"

Caitlyn hesitated, then she told Pomona about the incident with her eyebrows in *Herbal Enchantments* and the fiasco with the chocolate warts growing on Angela Skinner and her friends. She purposefully didn't mention the incident in the kitchen yesterday when the chocolate decorations had appeared, as if created by *her* imagination—that was another thing she didn't feel she could talk to her cousin about.

"I knew it! I knew there was witchcraft going on in that village! I told you so, didn't I?" said Pomona, sounding jubilant.

"It might not be witchcraft. It might be..." Caitlyn trailed off weakly, not able to come up with a good alternative.

"And I'll bet witchcraft was used in the murder too," continued Pomona as if she hadn't heard her. "The wife could have asked the Widow Mags to help her get rid of her husband and—"

"No, Amy wouldn't do that," protested Caitlyn. "I got chatting to her when she invited me back for coffee. She seems like a really sweet girl. I just can't see her as a murderer."

"Murderers can be very good at, like, hiding their real personas," said Pomona, in the superior voice of someone who had watched too many TV crime dramas. "Okay... maybe it wasn't Amy who asked the Widow Mags to poison her husband—maybe it was the Widow Mags herself! I mean, she's a witch, right? And if you've got the power to do things—you know, to punish bad people—wouldn't you be tempted to use it?"

"I..." Caitlyn hesitated, thinking of the chocolate warts that had appeared on Angela and her friends yesterday. It had been funny, yes, but didn't it also show that the Widow Mags wasn't afraid to use magic to get vengeance? And the old woman didn't care about following the rules of society—that had been obvious in that argument between her and Bertha. The Widow Mags lived by her own rules and if she wanted to get justice for a poor abused wife, would she really hesitate to use witchcraft to—

Caitlyn pulled herself up sharply. What was she thinking? This was ridiculous! Since when had she started thinking about using magic like it was real? Since when had she started believing that people could really hex others? The Widow Mags wasn't a witch—she was just a cranky old woman who made delicious chocolates!

"Caitlyn? Caitlyn? Are you still there?"

"Mmm... yes, sorry," Caitlyn mumbled.

"So when are you coming back?"

Caitlyn didn't answer for a moment, then she said: "Not for a while yet. I still haven't really had a chance to ask my own questions. The whole village has just been so preoccupied with the murder and stuff. Oh, but listen to this... the Widow Mags recognised my runestone!"

"She did?"

"Yes, I showed it to her yesterday—her and her daughter, Bertha—and they both looked really shocked. Like they recognised it. They know something, I'm sure of it—maybe they even know my mother. I tried to ask but the Widow Mags shut me down. But I'm going to try again. And until I get some answers, I'm not leaving Tillyhenge."

"But Caitlyn, don't you think—" There was a burst of static and Pomona's voice disappeared.

"Hello? Hello? Pomie, are you there?" Caitlyn lowered the phone and stared at the screen. It showed no signal. She sighed. It looked like she had lost the connection. She would have to try and call Pomona back later.

Getting out of bed, Caitlyn splashed some cold water on her face and dressed hurriedly, then ran down the spiral staircase. The chocolate shop was open but she couldn't see the Widow Mags out in front. Wandering into the rear of the cottage, Caitlyn thought she heard a sound coming from the kitchen. Actually, it sounded like it was coming from the stillroom, off to one side of the kitchen. It must have been the Widow Mags checking her supplies.

Hurrying into the stillroom, Caitlyn said, "Good morning... um... when you've got a moment, can I please talk to you about—"

She broke off in surprise when she saw who was in the stillroom. It wasn't the Widow Mags—it was Amy Matthews, and she had her hand up on one of the shelves. It looked like she was reaching up either to get something or return something to its place.

"Oh!" The young woman jumped in surprise and dropped whatever it was she had been holding. It hit the ground and rolled towards Caitlyn, who stooped to pick it up. It was a small glass vial with a label that said: "*BELLADONNA EXTRACT*". She raised her eyes to find herself looking at Amy's flushed, guilty face.

The other woman smiled brightly. "Heavens, you really startled me!"

"What are you doing here?" Caitlyn blurted.

"I... um... I came to find something to put on my bruises. I remembered the Widow Mags giving me something last time which really helped them heal faster. I thought I'd ask her for some more but I couldn't find her anywhere so I thought I'd just pop in here and have a quick look. I knew she wouldn't mind," Amy said breathlessly. "The last time I was here, she'd told me to come in and help myself whenever I needed something."

"Does belladonna help with bruising?" asked Caitlyn, frowning as she held the vial up.

Amy gave an uneasy laugh. "Oh, is that belladonna? I didn't realise. I must have misread the label. I was looking for arnica. The Widow Mags made a compress with it last time, which worked like magic... Ah, here it is".

Quickly, she whisked another vial off the shelf and held it up with a breezy smile. Caitlyn handed the vial of belladonna back to Amy and watched as the other woman reached up to replace it on the top shelf. She seemed very familiar with the room, her movements quick and sure.

"Um... well, I guess I'll go now..." Amy said, pocketing the vial of arnica. "If you see the Widow Mags, will you thank her f—"

She broke off as they heard a hubbub in the street outside. Caitlyn hurried out of the front of the shop, Amy at her heels. People were running down the lane, heading towards the village green. In the distance, she could hear a bigger uproar—like the sound of many raised voices.

"Hey!" she called at a lanky youth coming out of a cottage farther down the street. "What's going on?"

He gave her a wide-eyed look. "There's been another murder!"

CHAPTER FIFTEEN

Caitlyn ran with Amy towards the village green, bursting out into the open space to find a large crowd of people assembled outside the pub. Everyone was talking and gesticulating excitedly, then—as the crowd shifted and parted—Caitlyn saw the detective inspector from yesterday standing just outside the pub entrance. He was raising his hand for silence, and gradually the jabbering died away to be replaced by an uneasy anticipation.

Inspector Walsh cleared his throat and began speaking: "I am afraid I have bad news. The body of reporter Rob Wiggins was found a few hours ago. It appears that he was murdered."

"Murdered!"

"Oh my God, another one?"

"It's that witch—I know it's her!"

"We're all going to be murdered in our beds!"

"Please!" The inspector raised his voice. "I must ask you all to remain calm. There is no immediate danger to any other resident in this village."

"Is it the same person who killed Stan?" came a yell from the crowd.

"We believe that the same person may be responsible for the two deaths, yes," admitted the inspector.

"Do you know who it is?"

"Are you going to make an arrest?"

"We are still continuing with our investigation," said the inspector. "And I hope to have an update for you shortly. In the meantime, the best thing you can do to help us is to remain calm and answer any questions that we may have."

"I heard you arrested that old witch woman!" a voice piped up. "The Widow Mags! I saw your constables marching her into the pub."

Caitlyn felt a stab of alarm. Had they really arrested the Widow Mags?

All around her, the voices were rising again.

"I knew it! I knew it was her!"

"I always said that she was a witch!"

"That woman is a menace!"

"Did you hear what happened at the chocolate shop yesterday? They say she hexed Angela and her friends and gave them all warts!"

Gasps. "No, really? She needs to be put away—"

"Please!" The inspector held both hands up, palms

out. "Please, I must ask you not to indulge in unnecessary and unhelpful speculation! The Widow Mags is helping us with enquiries, yes, but she is not under arrest."

"Is she a suspect for the murder?" someone asked.

The inspector hesitated. "She is one of several people we are questioning. I will let you all know when we have further news. In the meantime, please come forward to speak to one of my constables if you have any information concerning Rob Wiggins or his murder. Now, if you'll excuse me…"

He turned and made his way back into the pub. Caitlyn hesitated a moment, then darted through the crowd until she arrived at the pub door. She expected the young policeman standing outside to turn her away but, when she gave her name, he said:

"Miss Le Fey? Inspector Walsh has been hoping to speak to you. If you can wait inside, I'll let the inspector know you're here."

Inside, Caitlyn found Bertha and Evie talking to a harassed-looking young sergeant.

"Ma'am, I can assure you, we are not mistreating your mother in any way. She is simply helping us with enquiries," said the sergeant. "She is not under arrest."

"Then why can't I see her?" demanded Bertha. "Why are you keeping her in the back room?"

"She's been detained while we conduct the necessary investigation into the latest murder—but it's only temporary. She'll be released as soon as we're satisfied we have all the information we require." He indicated one of the wooden booths. "If you'll take a seat, ma'am, we'll let you know as soon as you can see her."

He disappeared through the doorway leading into the private rooms at the back of the pub. Bertha heaved an angry sigh and sat down in the booth.

Evie hovered next to her. "Mum, why didn't you just do some magic to make him let you through to see Grandma?"

Bertha frowned at her. "I told you, Evie, you can't use magic willy-nilly for every problem!"

"I don't see why not," pouted Evie. "If you've got it, why not use it? It seems stupid not to take advantage of it. It's a perk, right?"

"No, it's not a perk—it's a gift," said Bertha severely. "And it shouldn't be taken for granted. It can be dangerous and addictive if you get too used to using it. Besides, you shouldn't be using magic to manipulate others against their will. That's—oh, Caitlyn, I'm so glad to see you here!"

Bertha sprang up, her face breaking into a smile of relief.

"What happened?" asked Caitlyn. "I know Rob Wiggins was murdered but why are they holding your mother?"

"I'm not sure," said Bertha with a sigh. "I think they found traces of chocolate on Wiggins's body. He was found up by the stone circle—it looks like he went there last night after leaving the pub, although no one saw him walking there. He was poisoned, just like Stan Matthews."

"With belladonna?"

"I think so. The police wouldn't tell me much." She paused, then asked, "Did you see my mother last night?"

Caitlyn shook her head. "No, she wasn't around when I got back from the pub after dinner. The back door of the cottage was open. I wondered if she'd gone out for a walk or something."

"Yes, she might have. She was very disturbed after seeing your... She had a lot on her mind."

"Miss Le Fey? Inspector Walsh will see you now."

Caitlyn turned to find the sergeant standing behind her. She gave Bertha a wan smile and followed the sergeant to the back of the pub. He showed her into a room at the end of the corridor. It was a small sitting room and the inspector was in an armchair, perusing some papers on his lap. But what made her stop short was the sight of James Fitzroy sitting in the other armchair, looking cool and elegant in a charcoal grey three-piece suit and a royal blue tie. He didn't acknowledge her as she came in and seemed content to sit in the background.

Inspector Walsh looked up. "Ah. Miss Le Fey— please, have a seat."

Caitlyn sat down, trying not to look at James.

"Now..." The inspector shuffled the papers and laid them aside, then leaned forwards and regarded Caitlyn with shrewd eyes. "I understand you're a lodger at *Bewitched by Chocolate*?"

"Um... yes, I've been staying there the last couple of days."

"May I ask why you chose to stay there?"

"There was no room at the pub so somebody suggested the chocolate shop."

"And can you tell me, when was the last time you saw the Widow Mags?"

"Er... well... it would be around six in the evening yesterday, I think. I was helping her clear up the mess in the shop."

The inspector raised his eyebrows slightly and Caitlyn felt obliged to explain.

"The Widow Mags has arthritis and it's hard for her to do certain things, so I thought I'd help out."

"That's extremely charitable of you," commented the inspector dryly.

Caitlyn shrugged. "I'm... I'm on vacation. I haven't got anything particular to do anyway."

"Still, it seems unusual... May I ask, what is the nature of your relationship with the Widow Mags?"

"The nature of our relationship...?" Caitlyn looked at him blankly. "What do you mean? I only met her the day before yesterday, when I arrived in Tillyhenge."

"And yet you are happy to devote so much of your holiday time to helping a stranger?" The inspector raised a disbelieving eyebrow. "One would think that there has to be some kind of prior relationship or connection between you...?"

"I don't know what you're talking about," said Caitlyn. "Haven't you ever helped a stranger in your life? Done something kind just because you could?"

"Hmm…" Inspector Walsh was silent for a moment, then he said, "And have you noticed anything strange or untoward during your time in the chocolate shop?"

Caitlyn swallowed. "You mean, like what Angela was saying about the chocolate warts—"

The inspector waved an impatient hand. "No, no, not that nonsense. I mean, something else. Something which might be pertinent to the murder case."

Caitlyn hesitated. "Well, I don't know if this is relevant but… the first night I was staying there, I woke up in the middle of the night. I looked out my window and saw a bonfire."

"A bonfire?"

"Yes, a large one. At the site of the stone circle."

"Ah…" Again, the inspector waved an impatient hand. "Yes, we know about that. Lord Fitzroy mentioned it. It's probably nothing. There have been some reports of arson in a few other villages in this area. A couple of teenage boys playing around with things they shouldn't. It's the summer holidays at the moment—kids are off from school, looking for trouble."

"Yes, but I don't think this is the same thing. This was in the centre of the stone circle and looked like… well, it looked like a ritual fire."

"Ritual fire?" The inspector's tone was sarcastic. "Miss Le Fey, I think you're letting your imagination run away with you. Don't let the local gossip give you ideas. There's been a long tradition of pagan beliefs and fascination with myths and legends in Tillyhenge. People are always quick to think of a supernatural cause—and especially with that stone circle nearby. I imagine it's profitable for them, what with all the tourists. You know, there are so many villages in the Cotswolds—they have to compete with each other for tourism and everyone wants to be unique. Tillyhenge is just trying to sell itself as the village with witchcraft and magical connections."

"But when I asked the local villagers about it, they all seemed to clam up! It was almost like they were hiding something—"

"Miss Le Fey." The inspector sounded bored now. "Let me assure you that the fire is nothing to worry about. Now," he said, changing the subject briskly, "I believe you were at the pub all evening last night?"

Caitlyn resisted the impulse to glance at James. "Yes, I had dinner there. With Hans van Driesen."

"Ah yes. Mr van Driesen..." Inspector Walsh trailed off meaningfully. "And did you see Rob Wiggins while you were at the pub?"

"Yeah, I did, actually. When I arrived, he was at the bar talking to Mr van Driesen. I think Rob Wiggins was interviewing him—he was busy writing notes. And then I saw him again later," added Caitlyn, remembering. "He came past our table just as we finished eating. I thought he looked a bit unwell. He asked if he could have my water and then gulped the whole glass in one go."

The inspector nodded. "Extreme thirst and a dry mouth are common symptoms of atropine poisoning."

Caitlyn stared at him. "Atropine? So Wiggins was definitely poisoned as well?"

"We'll have to wait for the toxicology analysis to confirm things but yes, on initial examination, the forensic pathologist believes that he was murdered by the same poison which killed Stan Matthews. Atropine, derived from extract of belladonna." Inspector Walsh paused, then added significantly, "And we also found traces of chocolate on his fingers. Again, it will have to be confirmed by tests but we believe it will match the chocolate found on Stan Matthews's body."

Caitlyn shook her head. "Come on, you don't really think that the Widow Mags murdered him? Or Stan Matthews?"

"I'm not thinking anything at the moment," said the inspector evenly. "I'm just gathering evidence. But I must say, right now, a lot of the evidence points towards the Widow Mags."

"She wasn't even at the pub last night!" said Caitlyn. "How could she have poisoned Rob Wiggins?"

"Depending on the dose, belladonna can be a slow-acting poison. It can take several hours for the symptoms to manifest." Inspector Walsh leaned back and added, his voice suggestive, "Rob Wiggins was at the chocolate shop earlier in the afternoon yesterday."

Caitlyn shook her head impatiently. "But it doesn't make sense—why would the Widow Mags want to kill a journalist? For that matter, why would she want to kill Stan Matthews? She's got no motive."

"Well, I've been speaking to Lord Fitzroy here and I believe she could have a very good motive," said the inspector, nodding towards James.

Caitlyn glanced across at him. James's face was carefully blank of all expression, his grey eyes shuttered.

She turned back to the inspector. "What do you mean?"

"She is very friendly with Amy Matthews, the gamekeeper's wife, isn't she? And I understand that Amy was being physically abused by her husband. As I suggested yesterday, it would be understandable if the Widow Mags felt compelled to help—"

"That's ridiculous!" said Caitlyn hotly. "You're suggesting that she would help someone murder their husband? The Widow Mags would never do that!"

Inspector Walsh raised her eyebrows. "Really? And yet yesterday, when I questioned her at the chocolate shop, she sounded like she would have been glad to help."

Caitlyn rolled her eyes. "That's just something

people say—like saying, 'I'll kill him!'—but they don't really mean it. The Widow Mags's bark is worse than her bite. I almost think she likes to say things just to shock people. She wouldn't really have done it."

"You seem very confident of knowing how she would act. And yet you've only known this woman... how many days did you say? Since the day before yesterday?" His tone was sarcastic.

Caitlyn flushed. "Well, I've spent quite a lot of time with her. And you... you get a vibe from someone."

"But yet you maintain that you never met her before. You say you have no prior history with her, no relationship, no other connection. So how can you know her so well?" asked the inspector. "We have interviewed several of the villagers and everyone seems to be scared of her. They all say that she's been in the village for as long as they can remember, and yet none of them really know much about her, beyond the fact that she makes chocolates. It seems strange, doesn't it, to have someone resident in a place for so long and yet to be so excluded from the community?"

"Well, there are loners everywhere. That's hardly news," said Caitlyn with a shrug.

"Perhaps. But in this case, she's not just a hermit living alone at the edge of the village—she's someone who is actively feared by the other residents." Inspector Walsh leaned forwards and said, "Look, Miss Le Fey, I don't know if you're telling the truth about having no connection to or history with the

Widow Mags. Perhaps you really are just an altruistic visitor who feels sorry for the old woman. Perhaps you think you need to protect her. But I can tell you, your loyalty is misplaced. If the Widow Mags is responsible for these murders, it's your duty to help me bring her to justice."

"You just want a scapegoat," Caitlyn accused him. "You want an easy solution to this murder—it's taking up too much space in the media, isn't it? It looks bad for the police not to be making any progress on the case or have any arrests. You want to wrap it up quickly so you're just doing the easy thing. The villagers don't like the Widow Mags so that gives you the perfect scapegoat. What about your other suspects? Have you questioned Mr van Driesen about his movements last night?"

"I'd thank you not to tell me how to do my job, Miss Le Fey," said the inspector testily. "Yes, we *have* questioned Mr van Driesen and he has been more than helpful. He provided us with a full account of his movements last night and we can verify that he was in the pub the entire time. By the time he returned to his room, Rob Wiggins would have already been dead."

"Yes, but you said yourself that belladonna is a slow-acting poison. Van Driesen was standing right next to Rob Wiggins at the bar counter—he could have easily slipped something into the reporter's drink. Maybe that was why he asked me to dinner!" said Caitlyn excitedly. "Maybe it was so he could have an alibi and not be with Wiggins when the reporter started showing symptoms of poisoning!"

"Hmm..." The inspector frowned. "That is—"

He broke off suddenly as they heard sounds of a great commotion coming from the front of the pub. It sounded like two fishwives having a screaming match.

"What the—!" The inspector sprang up and hurried from the room.

Caitlyn and James looked at each other for a second, then rushed together after him..

CHAPTER SIXTEEN

They stepped into the main room of the pub to find it filled with people screaming and shouting, fingers pointing, hands waving. The sergeant and two constables were struggling to keep order but they were being largely ignored by the group of women in the centre. Caitlyn saw that everyone was gathered around two ladies: Angela and Bertha, who were facing each other, looking like they were going to come to blows at any moment.

"QUIET!" thundered the inspector.

Everyone stopped, shocked into silence.

"Now, what is going on?" asked Inspector Walsh, glowering at everyone.

"I'll tell you, Inspector!" cried Angela, stepping forwards. She was clutching a Styrofoam cup filled with hot chocolate—not the thick, rich, home-made

DARK, WITCH & CREAMY

beverage served in the Widow Mags's shop, but a cheap, watery instant chocolate, full of sugar and artificial flavourings. Caitlyn could smell the sickly sweet fragrance wafting from the cup.

Angela drew herself up importantly. "I came to help you with the investigation. I have evidence to report."

Inspector Walsh raised his eyebrows. "Evidence?"

Angela nodded eagerly. "Yes. Evidence that the Widow Mags is the murderer."

Bertha gasped in outrage. "That's a load of—"

The inspector held a hand up, silencing Bertha. Then he turned back to Angela. "Very well, ma'am. If you could please tell me what you'd like to report?"

"Well! As you know, Inspector, I was at the chocolate shop yesterday afternoon and that old witch inflicted the most terrible curse on me—"

"Hmm, yes, we've been through that already, Miss Skinner," said the inspector irritably. "And as I told you yesterday, I'm afraid accusations that cannot be substantiated with concrete proof are not something the police can take action on."

"Oh, but that's not what I came here to tell you, Inspector," said Angela quickly. "What I wanted to say was that while I was at the chocolate shop yesterday, I noticed that Rob Wiggins was there. He was sitting in the window seat, having a hot chocolate."

"Yes, Miss Skinner, I was aware of that already," said Inspector Walsh, starting to lose patience.

"Ah, but what you don't know is that I saw the old woman put poison in his drink."

Caitlyn stared at Angela in disbelief whilst, next to her, Bertha gasped and spluttered with outrage.

"Do you have proof of this, Miss Skinner?" asked the inspector.

"You have my word, Inspector! How much more proof do you need? I'm telling you, I saw it with my own eyes: the Widow Mags added something from a vial into Rob Wiggins's hot chocolate, before she served it to him. And it wasn't just me. My friends saw it too." She turned to the ladies beside her and elbowed them roughly. "Didn't you?"

"Oh... er... yes! Yes, that's right—we saw it too," they said in unison.

Caitlyn narrowed her eyes. They were lying; she was sure they were lying. Angela must have put them up to it. She felt a surge of anger. She was sure the whole thing was a vindictive ploy because Angela wanted to get revenge for what the Widow Mags had done to her yesterday.

"It's a lie," Caitlyn spoke up suddenly.

Angela glared at her. "Are you calling me a liar?" she hissed.

Caitlyn looked at her evenly. "Yes, I am. The Widow Mags served Rob Wiggins his hot chocolate *before* you came into the store, so you couldn't have seen her doing anything. You're lying just to incriminate her."

"How dare you!" cried Angela, her face going red.

"Now, now, ladies..." said Inspector Walsh hastily. "There's no need to get worked up. Conflicting witness accounts are quite common. Everyone has a different view of the situation, depending on their own perspective and interpretation."

"I know what I saw!" snapped Angela. "Are you going to take the word of some stupid little tourist over mine? She's only been in the village a few days. What does she know?"

"I'm merely stating the truth," said Caitlyn.

"Oh really?" Angela put on an affected voice, mimicking Caitlyn's accent. "'I'm merely stating the truth'—so high and noble, aren't you? Just like yesterday when you paid for Amy Matthews's bread. Such a little do-gooder," she sneered, shoving her face into Caitlyn's.

Caitlyn felt the anger inside her surging even higher, boiling, furious. She wanted to shove something into that loud mouth, to stop the woman from talking. The cup of chocolate in Angela's hand frothed suddenly like an erupting volcano.

"Evie!" hissed Bertha, glaring at her daughter. "Stop that!"

"What?" cried Evie. "I'm not doing anything!"

Angela was still jeering at Caitlyn, oblivious, "...oh yes, you think you're so superior, don't you? Coming here and—"

The cup exploded, sending a miniature chocolate geyser shooting up into Angela's face, filling her mouth.

"—thinking you're better than everyo—*AUGH-BLUB-GGHH!... BLUB... BLUB... BLUB... BLUB...!*"

Angela staggered around, sounding like someone gargling in the shower. Giggles erupted from the crowd. It was such a funny sight: as if a garden hose of liquid chocolate had been turned on and directed at the woman's face.

Then, as suddenly as it started, the stream of chocolate shut off. Angela dropped the cup on the floor, choking and spluttering. Everyone gaped at her. She was covered in slimy brown liquid, with watery chocolate dripping off her chin and hair.

"*Evie!*" cried Bertha, staring at her daughter in horror.

"It wasn't me!" protested Evie, looking scared now.

Something in her daughter's face must have convinced Bertha and she turned back to look at the empty Styrofoam cup, now lying innocently on the floor, a few drops of chocolate leaking from its rim. Then, slowly, Bertha raised her eyes to Caitlyn, who was also staring at the cup, a mixture of emotions on her face.

"You!" shrieked Angela, pointing a finger at Caitlyn. "It was you! I knew it—you're a witch as well! You did it! You made the chocolate go ballistic on me!"

Caitlyn shook her head dumbly. She looked like someone who had just woken up from a dream. "It... I don't... I didn't mean..."

"Now, now, there's no need to get hysterical," said

Inspector Walsh, holding his hands up. "I'm sure there's a perfectly good explanation. Sometimes, these takeaway drinks are so hot that pressure builds up inside the cup and then, perhaps, if it is jolted suddenly, it might cause the liquid to burst out... similar to when a bottle of fizzy drink is shaken."

"But it wasn't hot anymore," Angela insisted. "It was barely lukewarm. If it had been hot, I would have been scalded but I'm not."

It was true. Everyone could see that. The only injury Angela had really suffered was to her pride. But Caitlyn knew what the inspector was trying to do: offer a rational explanation for something that otherwise could only be explained by one thing—magic.

Angela shoved her face close to Caitlyn's and hissed, "I don't care what anyone says. I know you did this and I won't forget it!"

Turning, she stormed out of the pub, followed by her friends.

CHAPTER SEVENTEEN

They were dismissed by the inspector and Caitlyn followed Bertha and Evie gratefully out of the pub. As soon as they were outside, however, Bertha grabbed her elbow and pulled her a safe distance away from the prying ears of the crowd still gathered in front of the pub.

"It was you, wasn't it?" she said, looking Caitlyn straight in the eye.

"I-I-I don't know what you mean," Caitlyn stammered.

"That thing with the hot chocolate exploding in Angela's face. You made that happen, didn't you?" She leaned towards Caitlyn, peering at her closely, then a smile spread slowly across her face. "I knew it. You are a witch."

"What? No, that's crazy! I'm not... I didn't—"

"Are you saying that you had nothing to do with what happened to Angela?"

"I... I don't know," Caitlyn admitted. "I just... I felt really angry, like... like this anger was boiling inside me and I just wanted her to shut up... and then the next minute... I don't know what happened but it was like my feelings transferred themselves to that cup of hot chocolate!"

Bertha nodded in satisfaction. "Yes. Exactly as I thought. You're a witch."

"I'm not a witch!" cried Caitlyn, shriller than she intended. She noticed people from the crowd turning to look at them and hurriedly lowered her voice. "I'm *not* a witch!" she repeated with emphasis. "Witches don't exist, there's no such thing as magic—it's all a bunch of old wives' tales and folk legends."

"Magic is simply the ability to cause change by force of will," said Bertha. "Those who can work magic have learnt to harness the energy in the universe and direct it with intent towards a certain purpose."

"I didn't intend to do anything to Angela," Caitlyn protested.

Bertha smiled. "Perhaps not consciously. But you felt angry and wanted to stop Angela talking—and your gift translated that emotion into action. You obviously have a strong natural ability, to be able to do that without conscious focus and without any training. Most witches have to practise for years before they have that kind of ability. And..." She looked thoughtfully at Caitlyn. "It's interesting that it was the hot chocolate you manipulated."

"Why is that interesting?"

"Well, there are different types of witches, you see. Oh, we can all learn to cast spells and brew potions—those are the basics—but each family is endowed with certain talents which run through the generations. Ours is an affinity with chocolate."

"With chocolate?" Caitlyn felt like laughing. "What, you guys are like the chocolate witches?"

Bertha gave her a reproachful look. "It's not a joke. Cacao is a potent source of magic. The ancient Mayans and the Aztecs knew about this. They called it *xocolātl*—'food of the gods'. Cacao beans were associated with wisdom and magical power, and the ancient witches and shamans used it in their spellworking rituals. They also understood its healing power." She laughed suddenly. "Why do you think people feel so good when they eat chocolate? It's not just the taste—there is something within chocolate itself, a dark and powerful magic which works on the mind and body. And the witches in my family have a gift for working with that magic." She reached out and patted Caitlyn's hand. "You are one of us, my dear."

Caitlyn opened her mouth to say something but nothing came out.

Bertha nodded, as if in answer to an unheard question. "I suspected as much from the first day I met you—I picked up a vibe from you. And there was the fact that you look so like..." She caught herself. "Well, anyway. And then I heard about those chocolate decorations you created, just naturally... and I knew."

Caitlyn stared at her. Was Bertha right? Could she really be a witch? And was this the answer to her questions about her past?

She licked dry lips. "Are you saying that I'm... that you are my family?"

Bertha hesitated. "That runestone—" She broke off as they heard a step behind them.

Caitlyn turned to see James Fitzroy standing next to them. She wondered how much he had overheard.

"Miss Le Fey... I was wondering if I might have a word with you?" he said, very formally.

"You go, dear," said Bertha quickly. "I need to nip back to my store to check something. I'll speak to you later. Come, Evie!" She bustled away, with Evie in tow.

Caitlyn followed James in a slight daze as he led the way over to a Range Rover parked at the side of the village green. Once again, she could feel the eyes of the villagers following them and knew that tongues must have been wagging. They reached the car and stood next to it awkwardly.

James cleared his throat. "I wanted to apologise for my manner in the pub last night."

Caitlyn looked at him in surprise. This was the last thing she had expected.

"I was concerned for your welfare and I may have

come across more... brusque than I intended."

"Oh. Um... that's okay," said Caitlyn. "I... uh... I'm sorry as well if I got a bit stroppy. I tend to lose my temper quickly sometimes." She gave a slightly shamefaced smile.

His eyes flicked to her red hair. "So it would seem. Was that another example in the pub just now with the hot chocolate?"

Caitlyn stared at him. Surely James Fitzroy wasn't suggesting that she was a witch too? "Wh...what do you mean?"

"What happened to Angela—it was some kind of prank, wasn't it? The cup was rigged to explode like that. Did you do that?"

Caitlyn stiffened. "I... no, I didn't..."

"Then do you know who did it? Was it Bertha or her daughter?"

"No!" said Caitlyn quickly. "Bertha and Evie had nothing to do with it."

James looked at her for a moment, an expression of frustration on his face. Then he sighed and said, "Caitlyn, I'm responsible for this village and its inhabitants. These are my people—I care about them. I care about what happens here in Tillyhenge. I need to know if anything... unpleasant is going on."

Caitlyn took a deep breath. "All I can tell you is that I... I didn't play a practical joke on Angela. And neither did Bertha and Evie."

He frowned, his expression still disbelieving. "Then what—"

SLURP!

Caitlyn yelped as she felt something wet and slimy rasp over her ear. She jerked around and saw— leaning out of the open back window of the Range Rover—an enormous English mastiff. It was Bran. He was panting amiably, his baggy face pulled back in a wide doggie grin, his pink tongue hanging out and drooling. The whole car was rocking from side to side, in time to his panting.

"Bran—no! Stop that," said James.

The big dog responded by giving the side of Caitlyn's head another loving lick.

"Eeuuw!" she cried, clutching her ear.

"I'm sorry!" said James, looking mortified. "Here, take this..." He handed her a crisp white handkerchief.

Caitlyn took it and wiped her ear, thinking that at this rate, she was going to end up with his entire handkerchief collection.

James made a face. "I'm sorry—Bran's been in the car the whole morning while I was at the pub with the police and he's probably a bit frustrated."

He opened the back door of the Range Rover and the mastiff jumped out. Caitlyn could almost feel the ground shake beneath her feet. Bran wagged his tail, then ambled over to Caitlyn, sat down on her left foot, and propped himself against her.

"Er... what's he doing?" she asked, staggering slightly under the huge dog's weight.

"Ah." James looked embarrassed. "Don't worry—

that just means he likes you. Mastiffs are leaners, you know. But he only does that to people he really likes."

"Oh... uh... well, I love him too, but can he get off my foot now? I think it's lost all circulation."

"Bran—get off the lady. Come on, get off, you big lump!" James shoved uselessly at the giant dog who sat, unmoving, looking at his master placidly.

At last, James straightened up, flushed and slightly dishevelled. "Er... he's very well trained, really. He just... needs a bit of time to think about the commands..."

"Yes, I'm sure," said Caitlyn, trying to keep a straight face. The sight of the handsome and dignified Lord Fitzroy struggling to move his big goof of a dog was just too funny.

A giggle escaped her lips in spite of her efforts; James caught her eye and gave her a rueful grin— then suddenly, they both burst out laughing. The sound of their laughter drew even more eyes from the crowd but Caitlyn didn't care. She couldn't remember the last time she had laughed like this.

"How's the kitten?" she asked at last, when they had both calmed down.

"It's doing fine—and in fact, 'it' is a he. A little boy. John, my stable master, thinks he's about six weeks old, only just weaned. But full of personality. Everyone's smitten with him—including me," said James with a chuckle. "Funny, I never thought I'd have a cat. I suppose sometimes life takes you by surprise." He gave her that lopsided smile, making her heart beat unsteadily. "You know, it's strange to think that everything only happened yesterday. I never imagined when I took Bran for a walk that I'd meet you at the stone circle and then end up falling in love."

Caitlyn felt her cheeks growing hot. She looked at him shyly, a tremulous smile on her lips. "R-really? I didn't... I didn't think that you would also fee—I mean, you must meet so many girls and I'm not really the glamorous type—"

"Er... I meant the kitten," said James, looking embarrassed.

Caitlyn flushed to the roots of her hair and squirmed. *Oh help.* She wished fervently for an earthquake and the ground to open and swallow her up—then she caught herself uneasily, wondering if that might really happen, considering what Bertha had told her about her witchy powers...

There was a sudden loud rumble and Caitlyn jumped. But it wasn't an earthquake. No, it was the sound of a throaty car engine. Caitlyn watched speechlessly as a gleaming red sports car slid into the village green and pulled up next to them. A beautiful girl with a deep tan, sun-kissed blonde hair, and designer shades sat in the driver's seat. She was chewing gum and nodding her head in time to the throbbing bass that was blaring from the car stereo. She beamed when she saw Caitlyn and waved madly.

Pomona jumped out of the car and ran over to give her a hug.

"Hi, Caitlyn! Surprise!"

CHAPTER EIGHTEEN

Everyone in the village green was staring wide-eyed at Pomona, with her tanned limbs exposed by her skimpy yellow sundress and her wavy blonde hair pinned up with an enormous satin flower. She looked like a tropical bird of paradise that had flown into an English farmhouse chicken coop.

Caitlyn groaned inwardly. She loved her cousin and was happy to see her but it was hard enough already trying to keep a low profile and not attract the attention of the villagers. Now with Pomona here, it was going to be impossible.

"Pomie! What you doing here?" she asked. "I thought you were in London?"

"We got cut off!" said Pomona, as if that explained everything. "I thought someone had come up behind you and, like, strangled you or something—"

Caitlyn gave her an exasperated look. "Yeah,

because that would be the natural thing to assume—as opposed to the phone just losing reception."

Pomona shrugged. "I had to check to make sure you were okay, you know? Besides, I was getting pretty bored in Oxford. I didn't go back to London—I decided to hang around for a while. Anyway..." She stole a glance at James, a coy smile on her lips. "Aren't you gonna introduce me to your friend, Caitlyn?"

Caitlyn groaned again. Of all the people she had to be talking to when Pomona arrived, it had to be James Fitzroy! With her cousin's overactive romantic imagination and penchant for matchmaking, she would never hear the end of it now.

"Pomona, this is... er... Lord James Fitzroy." She turned stiffly to James. "This is my cousin, Pomona Sinclair."

"*Lord* James Fitzroy?" Pomona squealed.

James smiled as he took her hand. "I hope you won't hold it against me, Miss Sinclair. Most people just call me James."

Caitlyn could see Pomona practically swooning at the sound of his sexy British accent. She grabbed her cousin's elbow and hastily began dragging her away. "Er... well, we'd better go now. C'mon, Pomie, I must show you the chocolate shop—"

Pomona ignored the attempts to move her, her eyes still glued to James. "Oh, please... call me Pomona," she said breathlessly.

"After the Roman goddess of fruits?" asked James,

quirking an eyebrow.

Pomona's eyes widened and she giggled. "Yeah! How did you know that? Most people have no idea."

James shrugged and gave a sheepish grin. "I read Classics at Oxford."

Pomona sighed loudly in delight and fluttered her eyelashes at him. James looked slightly unsure. Caitlyn rolled her eyes. She wanted to swipe her cousin across the head.

"*Ahem...* well, we mustn't keep you any longer, Lord Fitzroy. I'm sure you've got important matters to attend to." She looked pointedly at James.

He raised his eyebrows slightly at her use of his formal title but didn't comment. Instead, he gave them another of his heart-stopping smiles and said, "Right. Well, I'll see you around. And remember, you're welcome at the Manor to see the kitten anytime." He snapped his fingers. "Come on, Bran!"

He turned and began walking back towards the pub with the huge mastiff—for once obedient— following at his heels.

"Omigod! He's so *hot!*" squealed Pomona the minute he turned his back.

"Shhh! He'll hear you!" hissed Caitlyn, glancing towards James's retreating figure. The tips of his ears were red. *Oh heavens.* He had heard. She was going to die of mortification.

"So what? It's true!" said Pomona. "Did you see those shoulders? And those eyes? And that accent... Omigod! I thought I was gonna, like, melt into a puddle when he spoke to me..." Pomona gave a dramatic sigh and clutched at her heart, pretending to go weak at the knees.

"Stop it!" Caitlyn hauled her cousin back to her feet and started dragging her away from the village green, walking as fast as she could.

"He likes you, you know," said Pomona with a knowing smile.

"No, he doesn't!"

"Yes, he does. He's got it bad for you."

"Rubbish!" said Caitlyn, blushing furiously.

"Didn't you see the way he was looking at you? I know these things. I'm, like, an expert in lurrrve. That guy has fallen for you really bad. I would say that he's got the hots for you, except that would be too crass for someone like James Fitzroy. He's all classy and noble. He's like—" She mimicked a high-pitched English accent. "He 'holds you in high regard'..." She burst out laughing.

"Shut up," said Caitlyn, struggling not to laugh in spite of herself. "There's nothing between James and me—"

"Oooh! So it's *James* now, is it?" said Pomona, chuckling. "So tell me—how did you guys meet? Did he come across you while riding his big black stallion—"

"Pomie! This isn't a Jane Austen movie, okay? I just happened to meet him by the stone circle, that morning I went up there—"

"You never told me!" Pomona said accusingly.

"You were hiding it on purpose!"

"I wasn't hiding anything!" said Caitlyn. "I just didn't think it was important enough to mention. I mean, there was bigger stuff going on—like a murder."

"Honey, when you meet a man like that, it's always important enough to mention. Even when there's a murder," said Pomona, grinning.

They had arrived in front of *Bewitched by Chocolate* now and Caitlyn was relieved to see that the sight of the chocolate shop had finally distracted her cousin from the topic of James Fitzroy.

"Ohhhhh..." Pomona inhaled deeply as the rich cocoa aroma wafted out from the store. "Omigod, that is like the most delicious thing I have ever smelled..." She walked into the shop and stared around at all the chocolate on display. "I think I've died and gone to heaven."

Caitlyn smiled, feeling inordinately proud even though it wasn't her shop. She couldn't resist taking Pomona on a mini tour around the place and enjoyed watching her cousin's eyes glaze over as Pomona tasted the various creamy, decadent flavours.

"Stop, stop," said Pomona at last, waving her hand. "I think I'm gonna have a chocolate overdose! I'm gonna explode if I eat anymore!"

Caitlyn laughed and pulled her cousin through the doorway behind the counter into the rear of the cottage.

"This is the kitchen where a lot of the pieces are

created and—" Caitlyn broke off and stared at the huge black cauldron that was sitting in the fireplace at one end of the kitchen.

She blinked and rubbed her eyes. No, she hadn't imagined it.

There was a large ladle in the cauldron, which was filled with melted tempered chocolate. Caitlyn remembered the Widow Mags telling her that tempered chocolate had to be stirred continuously, to keep it from solidifying. So the ladle was nothing unusual—what was weird was the fact that nobody was stirring it. The ladle was going around and around by itself.

"Er... Caitlyn?" Pomona whispered, pointing at the stirring ladle. "What the...?" Then she gave a gasp and a squeal of delight. "Omigod, it's true! The old woman *is* a witch!"

She rushed over to the cauldron and stared down at it avidly, her eyes following the ladle around and around. "Omigod—I'm looking at honest-to-goodness, real-life magic!"

"Maybe there's some other explanation..." said Caitlyn weakly. "Maybe... maybe there's a mechanism at the bottom of the cauldron which attaches to the ladle and sort of moves it around..."

She trailed off as Pomona reached towards the ladle. Her cousin lifted it clear out of the swirling chocolate. It came up easily, dripping thick dark chocolate.

"Not attached to anything—see?" said Pomona.

She lowered the ladle slowly back into the cauldron and the two girls watched with bated breath. The ladle lay gently against the side of the cauldron for a moment, then—in front of their astonished eyes—it began moving around and around again, smoothly and steadily stirring the chocolate.

"It's true!" whispered Pomona, her eyes round. "It's enchanted—it *is* magic!"

Caitlyn looked at her cousin, amazed that Pomona could accept the concept of witchcraft and magic so calmly, so easily, when she herself had struggled with it so much. Why couldn't she have Pomona's easy faith?

She thought again of Bertha's insistence that she had the gift of magic in her blood, that she belonged to a family of witches... Could it be true? Did she dare believe it? Suddenly, Caitlyn felt a terrible longing to accept it, to embrace it. It would be so nice to feel like she wasn't alone anymore, to feel like she wasn't the only one who always felt "different", to have a real family to belong to...

Her thoughts churning, Caitlyn stared at the ladle going around and around. The more she stared at it, the more mesmerising it seemed. She took a step closer, feeling like she was being pulled towards the cauldron against her will. She leaned over and looked into the dark pool of rich, satiny chocolate. It seemed to get darker, deeper, the swirls smoothing out until it seemed like she was looking into a pool of dark glass.

She saw her own reflection for a moment, then it faded, to be replaced by the vague shape of trees... The forest behind the chocolate shop, Caitlyn realised... the outline of the trees silhouetted against the night sky, and the hill stretching up to the horizon ... and in the foreground... two figures climbing slowly up the hill...

Caitlyn gasped as she recognised one of them. It was Stan Matthews—she remembered seeing the framed photo of him at Amy's cottage the morning she had been invited for coffee. A dark figure walked beside him, a hand on Stan's shoulder, urging him up the hill, towards the stone circle ... Caitlyn frowned, leaning closer into the cauldron. Who was it? She could hear the rumble of their conversation—faint and muffled—like something coming from a distant room, through shut doors... Stan was gesticulating, talking, swearing, and the figure threw its head back and gave a deep belly-laugh...

Then a wave of chocolate swirled across the cauldron, blotting out the vision... and the next moment Caitlyn found herself staring once more at just a large cauldron of melted dark chocolate.

CHAPTER NINETEEN

Caitlyn stumbled backwards away from the cauldron, blinking and feeling slightly dizzy.

"Caitlyn? What happened?" asked Pomona.

"I... I saw..." Caitlyn gave her head a sharp shake, still not quite believing it. "I saw something in the chocolate..."

"In the chocolate?" Pomona looked puzzled. She glanced at the cauldron, then back at Caitlyn. "What did you see?"

Caitlyn gave a self-deprecating laugh. "It sounds crazy but I saw... I think I saw Stan Matthews walking with someone up the hill, towards the stone circle... I think it was the night he was murdered."

Pomona gave a squeal of delight. "It was a vision, Caitlyn! You had a vision!" She grabbed Caitlyn's hand and jumped up and down excitedly. "Omigod, this means that you could have the power too. You could be a witch!"

Again, Caitlyn was amazed at how easily her cousin accepted things. She wondered if she should reveal what Bertha had told her—about her witch heritage—then changed her mind. Instead, she said, "I thought people saw visions in crystal balls and things—not a bowl of chocolate!"

"Well, anything can be used for divination, really," said Pomona. "It's true that crystal balls are often used but that's only 'cos they have, like, a reflective surface. It's not like they're magic themselves or anything. In fact, you know the early witches used to use pools of water to help them see visions... and then later, they started using dark mirrors made of black glass or polished obsidian." She glanced back at the cauldron of gleaming dark chocolate. "I'll bet the chocolate took on the properties of a dark mirror! It doesn't really matter what it is, as long as the witch has the gift of sight and can, like, channel her visions through the reflective surface."

"How d'you know all this?" asked Caitlyn in amazement.

"I read," said Pomona smugly. "You know how much I love reading about magic and witchcraft and pagan spirits and stuff like that." She squeezed Caitlyn's hand excitedly. "Omigod, I can't believe that you could actually be a witch, Caitlyn! I've been trying to learn divination for years and never even come up with so much as a little déjà vu—and you go and have a whole vision the very first time. And about a murder, no less!" She gasped. "Did you see anything that could be a lead to the killer?"

"I don't know what I saw," said Caitlyn, rubbing her forehead. "I... It was all really hazy and I wasn't even sure at first what I was seeing... I saw Stan Matthews—I knew it was him—but the other person..."

"Was it a man or a woman?"

"I don't know," said Caitlyn helplessly. "It... it could have been either. I really couldn't tell. It was just a dark figure."

"Hmm... well, maybe—"

"Hullo? Anyone home?" a cheerful voice called from the front of the cottage.

The two girls returned to the shop and Caitlyn was surprised to see David Allan poking his head through the doorway. His eyes widened with admiration when he saw Pomona and he became very flustered.

"Oh! Sorry..." He fumbled with his briefcase. "I didn't realise you were with a friend..."

"This is my cousin, Pomona," said Caitlyn with a smile. "She's just visiting."

"Hiya," said Pomona, giving him a wink.

"H-h-hi," David Allan stammered, dropping his briefcase. It fell to the floor and burst open, scattering papers and stationary everywhere. "Oh!" he cried, flushing. "Sorry... s-so clumsy of me!" He crouched down and began gathering the spilled contents.

"Hey, let me help you," said Pomona, kneeling down next to him.

David became even more flustered, picking things up several times and then dropping them again. "Oh... that's... that's really kind of you... There's no need... Sorry, so clumsy of me..."

"Boy, you've got everything here but the kitchen sink," commented Pomona as she collected tissues, paperclips, packets of gum, pens, anti-bacterial hand gel, eye drops, disposable razors, discount coupons, and half an egg sandwich, and placed them back in the briefcase.

"I... er... I'm on the road a lot... so I find it's good to have things with me... to be prepared, so to speak..." David laughed nervously.

"I'll say," said Pomona, holding up a condom packet and giving him another wink.

David flushed even redder. "Th-those are not mine! I don't know how they got into my briefcase! I certainly wouldn't need... I mean, not that I don't have the opportunity... er... I mean..."

He looked like he was going to faint. Caitlyn was torn between laughing and feeling sorry for him. She could see that he was completely dazzled by Pomona—which wasn't a surprise. Caitlyn had seen the effect her glamorous cousin had on men many times before, and someone as shy and simple as David Allan had no hope of resisting Pomona's charms.

When everything was finally restored to the

briefcase and it was securely shut up again, David stood there, staring at Pomona with a rapturous expression, until Caitlyn cleared her throat and said:

"Can I help you, David? I'm afraid the Widow Mags isn't here."

He started and tore his eyes away from Pomona. "Oh! Er, actually... I really came for another cup of that delicious hot chocolate. I've never tasted anything like it. I've been thinking about it all day." He blushed as if admitting a guilty secret and glanced at Pomona.

"Well, I'm not sure if..." Caitlyn glanced at the empty counter, where the old woman would normally be presiding, then, making a split minute decision, she said, "I'm sure the Widow Mags would be happy for me to serve you a cup. Why don't you sit down?"

She grabbed a mug from the shelf behind the counter and, remembering how the Widow Mags had done it, filled it with some of the thick hot chocolate that was bubbling away on the small cauldron behind the counter (she was relieved to see that this one didn't have a magical stirring ladle).

"Here, I'll take it over," said Pomona, whisking the mug out of her hand and sashaying over to David, who was sitting at the window seat again.

Caitlyn watched her cousin lean against the wall next to David and start chatting and flirting with him, while the poor man hung on to her every word like an eager puppy. When Pomona finally turned to leave, he looked like he desperately wanted to ask her to join him but didn't have the courage. Instead, his eyes lingered wistfully over Pomona's curvy form as she sauntered back to the counter.

Caitlyn gave her cousin a mock frown and said in an undertone, "Pomie…"

"What?" Pomona giggled. "He's sweet. I like him."

"Yeah, and he's no match for you. So go easy on him, okay? I know what you can be like."

Pomona opened her eyes wide. "Me? What do you mean?"

Caitlyn gave her a stern look. "Pomie, you know I love you, but you're a heartbreaker. You love 'em and leave 'em. That might be okay for the guys you hang out with in Hollywood—they're used to that game—but David Allan's different. He's a nice guy. It would be cruel."

"Aww, I'm only having a bit of fun," said Pomona, pouting playfully. "Besides, how do you know? I might fall in love with him."

Caitlyn rolled her eyes. "Yeah? Since when? You have a taste for 'bad boys'. You're the one who's always telling me that nice guys are boring."

"Well, a girl has the right to change her mind, doesn't she?" said Pomona airily.

They were interrupted by new voices and Caitlyn looked up to see several tourists entering the shop.

"Hey—is this the place where we can get chocolate warts?" one of them asked eagerly.

"Er… chocolate warts?" said Caitlyn nervously.

"Yeah, it's been going around Facebook. Sounded

really cool. We just had to come and check it out."

Caitlyn's mind raced as she wondered how to answer him. How was she going to protect the Widow Mags now? Could she hide the truth about the old woman's witch abilities? Then to her astonishment, Pomona suddenly stepped forwards, gave the tourists a beaming smile, and opened her arms in a welcoming gesture.

"Yes! Come in! Come in! The chocolate warts were yesterday's special but we've got lots of cool new things in the store." She gave Caitlyn a wink, then turned back to the tourists and continued blithely, "Come in and take a look! You never know—you might discover today's magical chocolate experience!"

Caitlyn stared open-mouthed at her cousin as the tourists surged into the shop, chattering and pointing excitedly, grabbing things off the shelves, admiring the truffles and chocolate bonbons on display...

Pomona hurried behind the counter and grabbed a pair of tongs. "Okay, who would like to taste some delicious chocolates?" she said with a wink.

"Me!"

"Me!"

"Me too!"

"Me!"

For the rest of the afternoon, the two girls were rushed off their feet as more and more people arrived at the store. It seemed that somehow Angela's attempts to besmirch the Widow Mags's reputation had backfired on her. Instead, the "chocolate warts" had gone viral and become a social media sensation, and people were flocking to Tillyhenge to check out *Bewitched by Chocolate*.

"Jeez, you should tell the Widow Mags she needs to start making more chocolate body parts," said Pomona as she fielded yet another enquiry about chocolate warts. "Who knew people were so into random organs made of milk chocolate?"

Caitlyn laughed and pushed her hair back from her forehead, leaving a smear of chocolate in its place. She was doling out mugs of hot chocolate from behind the counter like a pro now, her movements slick and precise.

"Oh my Goddess, what have you girls been doing?"

Caitlyn turned to see Bertha standing in the doorway behind the counter, looking surprised and delighted as she saw all the customers in the store. Evie hovered behind her mother. They had obviously come in through the back door of the cottage.

"I finished for the day and thought I'd come and check on the chocolate shop, since I knew Mother's been stuck with the police all day," explained Bertha.

Caitlyn realised suddenly that it was past five o'clock and most shops would be closing. Where had the day gone?

"I hope your mother won't mind," she said quickly. "I was showing my cousin, Pomona, around the store and some customers arrived so we thought it would be a shame to turn them away—"

"Mind? She'll be bloody delighted!" said Bertha, beaming. "I don't think I've ever seen the shop this busy!"

"But it could be like this all the time!" said Pomona eagerly, coming to join them. "There's so much potential here! Half the things aren't even being displayed properly—and it's, like, so dark and gloomy in the store. You need to brighten the place up and put some things in the windows and make some displays..."

"I couldn't agree more," said Bertha, nodding emphatically. "I've been trying to tell my mother that until I'm blue in the face but will she listen to me?" She rolled her eyes. Then she smiled. "Maybe now that you girls have shown what can be achieved, she might be more willing to listen."

"Oh, I'd love to give the shop a makeover!" said Pomona, her eyes sparkling. "I would repaint the walls and add some fake torches in gold sconces to the walls—you know, play up the whole Mayan-Aztec thing—and have some of those cacao pods painted in gold and stacked in the window, together with a display of truffles and chocolate bars and some chocolate sculptures... Man, the chocolates in here are so gorgeous, if people could just *see* them, I'm sure they'd come in!"

"Your ideas sound wonderful," said Bertha. "I just hope you can convince my mother to let you do them."

A familiar grumpy voice growled suddenly behind them: "Do what? What are you planning to do to my shop?"

CHAPTER TWENTY

They turned to see the Widow Mags standing in the doorway behind the counter. She too must have come in through the rear door of the cottage. And with her was James Fitzroy, who kept a solicitous hand under the old woman's elbow as she leaned heavily on her stick and hobbled through the doorway to join them.

"I'm all right! Don't fuss!" The Widow Mags shrugged him off irritably.

"Mother, we thought the police were holding you overnight!" said Bertha, hurrying over to her.

The old woman made a dismissive wave in James's direction. "Lord Fitzroy spoke to that fool of an inspector—gave his word for me."

Caitlyn glanced at James. The Widow Mags couldn't have sounded more ungrateful, but James simply looked amused, obviously used to the old woman's cantankerous manner.

"What are all these people doing here?" demanded the Widow Mags, gesturing to the customers in the shop as if they were intruders who had broken into her store.

"Those *people* are customers, Mother," said Bertha in exasperation. "And Caitlyn and her cousin have worked a miracle! I've never seen the shop do such good business. They've got some wonderful ideas for making the shop look better—especially Pomona here." She pushed the girl in front of her.

Pomona gulped. Now that she was suddenly face to face with a woman who looked exactly like a storybook witch, she was speechless.

"Are you saying my chocolate shop is ugly, girl?" asked the Widow Mags, glowering at Pomona.

"N-n-no, ma'am! N-no, I mean... It's j-just that... Well..." Pomona hesitated, then she swallowed and raised her chin, looking the old woman straight in the eye. "A-actually, yes, I am."

There was a stunned silence.

Then the Widow Mags gave a sudden cackling laugh. "So, you have spirit, eh, girl? I like that!"

Pomona stared at her, then gave a hesitant smile. Everyone relaxed.

"Tell me again what you want to do to my shop?" the Widow Mags said to Pomona.

"It's called a makeover," said Pomona excitedly, and she began telling the Widow Mags all her ideas and plans. When she'd finished, the old woman was silent for a moment, then she gave a single nod.

"All right, do your 'makeover'," she growled. "But I warn you, if I don't like it, I want everything put back the way it was—down to the last cobweb!"

"Yes, ma'am!" Pomona giggled and gave her a mock salute. Then she turned eagerly to Caitlyn and Evie. "Let's start as soon as the shop closes. We can dust all the shelves and clean the..."

"Well, it looks like you ladies are going to be busy," said James with a smile. "I'll take my leave now. Goodnight."

"Lord Fitzroy."

He stopped and turned around. "Yes?"

The Widow Mags inclined her head—a slow, regal movement, as if she was a queen. "Thank you."

"Not at all. It was my pleasure."

He included them all again in his smile, then turned and strode out of the chocolate shop. Pomona sighed dreamily as he left.

"He's so gorgeous, isn't he?" said Evie. "If he wasn't so much older than me, I'd be totally going after him."

"I don't think it would do much good anyway," said Pomona with a grin. She elbowed Caitlyn. "I don't think anyone will stand a chance while this one's around."

"Shut up!" said Caitlyn, knowing she was blushing but unable to stop.

Evie turned wide eyes on her. "Ooh, really? You

mean, Lord Fitzroy likes—"

"No, Pomona's just making stuff up," said Caitlyn quickly. The village gossips were bad enough already without adding more fuel to the fire. Hastily, she changed the subject. "Okay, Pomie, what did you say you wanted us to do first?"

As soon as the shop closed, Bertha and the Widow Mags retreated to the kitchen while the three girls rolled up their sleeves and got out the mops, dusters, and brooms. Silence fell in the shop as they got to work sweeping, dusting, scrubbing, and wiping.

Pomona looked up from where she was cleaning the glass counter, examined her nails, and grumbled, "Cleaning sure isn't as fun as it looks in Disney cartoons. Look at my manicure! It's ruined!" She sighed. "Why can't we have, like, a bunch of forest animals or cute mice to magically clean the place for us?"

Evie put down the broom. "Hey, you know what? We can!"

"Huh?" Pomona looked at her.

"Well, not the forest animals bit—Unferal Spells are an advance level and I haven't done that. But I'll bet I can enchant the brooms and mops and get them to do the work for us!"

"Really? That would be so cool!" said Pomona eagerly.

"Wait, wait," said Caitlyn, thinking nervously of her monobrow experience in *Herbal Enchantments*. "Are you sure that's a good idea? I mean, your spells don't always... er... work out exactly the way you planned, Evie—"

"Oh, but this is easy," said the girl carelessly. "I've seen Mum do it lots of times—when she thinks no one is looking. She uses magic to get the housework done. It's so unfair! Parents are always like that—not letting you do stuff and then doing it themselves. I mean, I'm always telling her, the whole point of knowing witchcraft is to use—"

"Yes, but your mother's... um... an experienced witch," said Caitlyn, trying to be tactful.

"Oh, let the girl do some magic," said Pomona irritably. "Anything's better than having to scrub all this ourselves."

Caitlyn watched with apprehension as Evie stepped into the centre of the room and cleared her throat importantly.

"*Ahem!*" she said. She waved her hands, like a conductor directing an orchestra, and chanted:

"Dust to dust;
On curtains and sashes;
Sweep it all clean;
Before my eyelashes!"

For a moment, nothing happened. Then Caitlyn saw the bristles of the broom quiver. The next moment, it sprang up like it had been electrocuted and began moving back and forth over the floor, sweeping manically. On the walls around them, the rags began busily shuffling across the shelves, wiping all the dust off, and behind them, the mop plunged into the bucket, did a little twirl, then hopped out and began dancing across the floor.

"Oh my Goddess, it worked!" whispered Evie, looking as shocked as the other two girls.

"This is *soooo* awesome!" cried Pomona, beaming.

Even Caitlyn had to admit that it was pretty cool watching all the cleaning equipment do the hard work for them. The three of them stood grinning and enjoying the show. Within twenty minutes, the shop was immaculate, the glass counter sparkling, the wooden floors scrubbed clean.

"Evie, you're a genius," said Pomona.

The teenage girl flushed with pleasure. She raised her arms again and chanted:

"Spick and span,
Now stop you can!"

The mop obediently flopped to the floor, the rags fell together into a heap, the scrubbing brushes lined up in an orderly row, and the feather duster floated to the counter. Only the broom kept on sweeping.

"Er... Evie? That one's still going," said Caitlyn, pointing at the broom.

Evie frowned, raised her arms, and repeated the spell. The broom just started sweeping even faster. Evie tried again. Now the broom was almost manic as it zoomed around the room.

"Okay, now this is scaring me," said Pomona, watching wide-eyed. "Get it to stop."

"I'm trying!" said Evie. She screwed up her eyes, mumbled something under her breath, then pointed at the broom and said, *"So mote it be!"*

The broom froze for a moment, then turned and rushed towards Pomona and began shoving itself against her.

"Hey!" cried Pomona. "It's... it's trying to sweep *me!*"

The broom shoved and pushed, hustling Pomona across the room until she was standing next to Evie, then it shot the other way and began pushing at Caitlyn. She winced as the prickly bristles scratched her bare legs. Reluctantly, she found herself being herded across the room towards the other two girls, like a wayward sheep being herded back to the flock. In fact, the broom was acting a bit like a crazy sheepdog, darting in circles around her, jabbing at her with its handle to hurry her along, then dashing over to weave around the other two girls, before returning to hustle her again. She half expected it to start barking.

"Evie, what have you done?" demanded Caitlyn.

"I don't know!" wailed Evie as the broom nudged them all together, then swept happily around their ankles for good measure. She tried to make a run for the door but was herded unceremoniously back by the bristling broom.

"I don't believe this. We're being held hostage by a

broom," said Pomona.

Caitlyn didn't know whether to laugh or cry. "I'm going to call your mother—or your grandmother. They'll be able to stop it," she said to Evie, taking a deep breath to shout to the kitchen.

"No!" cried the girl. "Mum will tell me off for trying to use magic! Oh, it's so unfair! I could have shown her that I *can* work spells—and now she'll just think that I messed up again."

"Well, you'd better come up with *some*thing quickly," said Pomona, leaning away from the broom, which was trying to cuddleup against her. "Mr Broom here is getting *way* too friendly for me..."

"Wait, I have an idea," said Caitlyn. She stretched towards the counter behind them and snagged a bag of chocolate buttons. Quickly, she opened it and shook the contents of the bag into her hand, then raised her arm and flung them as far away across the room as she could. The chocolate buttons hit the floor and scattered in several directions.

The broom froze, then turned and rushed across the room to start manically sweeping up all the chocolate buttons.

"Quick! Quick! Let's get out of here!" cried Caitlyn, shoving the other two girls towards the rear of the cottage.

They stumbled and ran and burst through into the kitchen. The Widow Mags and Bertha looked up in surprise.

"Are you girls finished already?" said Bertha with

a smile. "That was quick." Then her gaze sharpened and she looked at her daughter suspiciously. "You used magic, didn't you?"

"Er... well..." Evie shifted uncomfortably, darting a look at the other girls.

Bertha walked past them and out to the front of the cottage. The three girls turned around and followed her back to the shop area, peering fearfully over her shoulder.

"My... I have to say, the place looks fabulous," said Bertha, smiling with approval. Then she spotted the broom still sweeping in a frenzy. "Ah! You left one of them running..." She snapped her fingers and the broom quivered, then sank slowly to the ground.

The three girls breathed a huge sigh of relief. They grinned at each other behind Bertha's back.

"It was all Evie's doing," said Pomona with a smile. "She's got, like, serious witch powers, man!"

"Well done," said Bertha, looking at her daughter proudly.

"Um... thanks. I... I had help," mumbled Evie. "Caitlyn and Pomona were great as well."

Bertha herded them back into the kitchen. "Well, you all deserve a treat. Come on, girls—it's time for dinner. You must be starving!"

Caitlyn suddenly realised that she could smell the most mouth-watering aromas drifting from the kitchen. Obviously, Bertha and the Widow Mags had been busy in their own way while the girls cleaned.

They trooped into the warm, cosy kitchen and

found the big wooden table in the centre laid with a smorgasbord of delicious home-cooked dishes: a plump brown chicken roasted to perfection with creamy dauphinoise potatoes and buttery parsnips, crispy pork belly with fennel, apple and minted baby peas, salty grilled sardines tart with fresh lemon and thyme, and a traditional cottage pie, the mashed potato coating fluffy on the inside and crispy golden on the outside—all accompanied by a refreshing salad of watercress, dandelion, goat's cheese, and walnuts.

"Omigod, as if the chocolate wasn't bad enough..." said Pomona with a groan as she eyed the table. "I'm going to put on twenty pounds by the end of the week!"

"Surely you didn't cook all this in twenty minutes?" said Caitlyn, staring at the table.

"Well... like you girls, we found that sometimes it helps to use a little bit of magic," said Bertha with a wink.

Everyone laughed and they sat down to the meal. A happy, rowdy atmosphere permeated the room; everybody seemed to be talking at the same time, calling to each other to pass the dishes, exclaiming over the flavours, sharing jokes and laughter.

Caitlyn sat back and let it all wash over her like a wonderful warm shower. She had never experienced family meals like this. Barbara Le Fey had been kind but always distant and preoccupied, making absent-minded replies to Caitlyn's attempts at conversation and rarely showing much interest in anything beyond her music and their upcoming travels.

Now Caitlyn looked at Bertha and the Widow Mags, bickering as usual, and at Evie, arguing passionately with Pomona about whether British men were sexier than American men, and she wondered wistfully what if it would be like if *this* was her family...

CHAPTER TWENTY-ONE

As they were finishing up dessert—stewed Cox apples with cinnamon sugar and home-made vanilla ice-cream—and leaning back contentedly in their chairs, the conversation turned serious at last and returned to the subject of the murder. *Murders*, Caitlyn reminded herself. There were two now.

"I think it's definitely that South African hunter dude," said Pomona. "The van Driesen guy. I mean, come on—the man's used to killing animals, right? So he wouldn't hesitate to do it."

"It's a big step from killing animals to killing humans," said Caitlyn.

Pomona looked at her in surprise. "Don't tell me you like the guy."

Caitlyn paused, then said, "I'm not saying Hans van Driesen is good or anything but... well, he didn't

206

apologise for what he was. He wasn't trying to be a hypocrite. I kind of liked that."

"But you don't agree with him about hunting the deer and other animals, do you?" gasped Evie, staring at Caitlyn in horror.

"No, no, of course I don't," said Caitlyn. "But us disapproving isn't going to stop people like him doing it. All I'm saying is, I liked the way he was upfront with me."

"Maybe he wasn't really being upfront—maybe it was a double bluff," said Pomona. "You know, like, come over all nice and cooperative... like, 'Yeah, I'm a hunter—I've got nothing to hide'..." Pomona held up her hands in a gesture of surrender. "And actually, it's all just an act."

"I agree with Pomona," said Bertha. "I don't think Mr van Driesen can be trusted."

"Hmm... where would van Driesen get the poison though?" pondered Pomona.

"James—I mean, Lord Fitzroy," Caitlyn corrected herself quickly, flushing, "—told me that atropine is used in lots of different drugs, like in eye drops and medications for excessive sweating, and it's also used to treat slow heartbeats. Oh, and also as an antidote for other poisons."

"Sounds like someone medical could get his hands on the poison really easily," said Pomona. "Van Driesen isn't, like, a pharmacist or a doctor, is he?"

Caitlyn shook her head. "No, he's a property

developer back in South Africa. Builds big tourist resorts and that sort of thing."

Pomona sighed. "Well, I guess we'd better leave it to the police—they'll figure it out eventually."

"No," said the Widow Mags, speaking up for the first time. "No, we cannot just leave it to the police. There is something... evil about these murders. Something motivated by more than just greed for money."

"Yes," Bertha agreed. "Yes, I feel like there is something very... intense and personal about these killings."

"To escape an abusive husband would be very personal," said Caitlyn softly.

Everyone turned scandalised eyes on her.

"You're not suggesting that Amy Matthews might be the murderer?" gasped Bertha. "Why, the poor girl is a victim herself!"

"That doesn't mean she can't be a killer as well," Caitlyn pointed out reluctantly. "She would have a really strong motive and the best opportunity. I mean, the autopsy report showed that Stan Matthews had chocolates in his stomach, right? And we know he had supper just before going to the pub. Well, who else other than his wife would have been in the best position to give him some chocolates laced with poison straight after dinner?"

"But where would *she* have got the poison from?" asked Pomona.

Caitlyn looked guiltily around. "I didn't really want

to mention this but... I found Amy in the stillroom this morning."

"I told her to come and help herself from my stillroom whenever she likes," growled the Widow Mags. "She was probably there to get something for her bruises. The poor child is covered in them."

Caitlyn swallowed. "Yes, that's what she said... but... when I saw her, she was reaching for a vial of belladonna."

"Are you sure?" The Widow Mags gave her a hard look.

Caitlyn wanted to shrivel under that fierce gaze but she forced herself to meet the old woman's eyes. "Yes. Amy dropped the vial and I picked it up. I read the label."

"No! I can't believe it!" said Bertha, sounding distressed. "I'm sure you're wrong! Maybe she was looking for something else and took the wrong vial off the shelf by mistake. We've all done that, especially when it's on a high shelf and you can't see the labels very well."

Caitlyn sighed. "I like Amy too and I don't want to believe it could be her either. But you can't eliminate someone as a suspect just because you like them. And... and you have to admit that she had the perfect motive and opportunity to poison Stan Matthews."

"What about the reporter guy?" asked Pomona. "If you think Amy is the murderer, then she must have poisoned Rob Wiggins too."

"She was standing very near him at the bar in the

pub. And it was really crowded in there, with a lot of people moving around. It would have been really easy for her to sidle up to him and add a couple of drops of belladonna to his pint of beer when he wasn't looking. In fact..." Caitlyn swallowed uncomfortably. "Maybe that's why she was in the stillroom this morning. She was returning the vial of belladonna."

"I still can't believe that such a sweet, nice girl could be a murderer!" Bertha burst out. "What about Mr van Driesen? He was in the pub too."

"Yes, you're right. And he was standing next to Rob Wiggins when I saw him," Caitlyn admitted. "So yes, he could have added the poison to Wiggins's beer too. But where would *he* have got the poison? Like we said, he doesn't have access to belladonna or atropine."

"Aarggh, we're going around in circles," said Pomona in frustration. "I think—" Whatever she was going to say was lost in a huge yawn. "Oh, sorry! Excuse me," she said, covering her mouth and looking sheepish.

Bertha smiled at her. "Don't be—you've had a long day, what with all the driving and then manning the shop all day and cleaning it as well! No wonder you're knackered!" She leaned forwards. "I hope you're not planning to drive back to Oxford tonight? It's nearly ten o'clock."

"You know, I hadn't thought about it," said Pomona, rubbing her eyes tiredly. She gave another yawn. "Is there, like, a couch somewhere I could crash on for the night?"

"I've got something better than that," said Bertha, smiling warmly. "We've got a spare bed in Evie's room. It's a bunk bed but it will be a lot more comfortable than a couch."

"You can have the upper or the lower bunk— whichever you like," offered Evie. "I'll take the other one. I don't mind."

"Thanks. That's really nice of you," said Pomona.

"In fact," said Evie eagerly, "I know of a spell which can grow your bed! We can try it when we get back. You'll just have to lie in your bunk and I'll turn it into a king-size luxury mattress around you and—"

"Er... I don't think you want to try any more spells tonight," said Caitlyn.

"Yeah," Pomona agreed in an undertone. "I'll probably end up turned into a hot dog and my bed into a bun... or worse!"

"Come on," said Bertha, getting to her feet. "We'll help clear up and then we'll be on our way."

***

Caitlyn opened her eyes and lay for a moment, staring up at the ceiling. The events of yesterday came rushing back to her, tumbling together like bits of coloured paper in a kaleidoscope: finding Amy in the stillroom... Rob Wiggins's murder... the interview with Inspector Walsh... Angela and the exploding hot chocolate... laughing with James... Pomona arriving in Tillyhenge... the busy afternoon serving customers in the chocolate shop, followed by the crazy sweeping broom and the wonderful family dinner...

But one memory stood out, sharper than the others: Bertha looking at her solemnly and saying, *"You're a witch, Caitlyn... you're one of us..."*

Caitlyn sat up abruptly and slid out of bed. She walked over to the window and looked out. The sky was still a pale blue-grey. Dawn had barely broken. But she knew that she wouldn't be able to go back to sleep now. She was too wide awake, too restless.

Washing and dressing quickly, Caitlyn tiptoed down the spiral staircase and let herself out the back door of the cottage. She breathed deeply as she stepped into the morning air. In the distance, she could hear birds twittering—the end of the dawn chorus—and everywhere was that fresh, clear feeling of a brand new day. A movement above her head made her glance up: she saw tiny dark shapes fluttering across the sky. They were too quick and small to be birds... *bats*, she realised. Heading home to roost now that the night was over. There must have been a bat colony that lived somewhere in the forest.

She would go for walk, Caitlyn decided. Up to the stone circle. She had wanted to visit it again and the exercise might help to get rid of some of her restlessness. There were two paths that led to the top of the hill: one on the open slope and a roughly parallel path that ran through the forest. She had taken the path on the open slope the first day—she decided to take the forest path now.

As she walked deeper and deeper into the woods, however, Caitlyn began to regret her decision. The morning light struggled to penetrate the canopy and there were deep shadows between the trees. Several times, she jumped and whirled at the sound of rustling or snapping twigs, only to remind herself that it was probably just some woodland creature scurrying through the undergrowth.

Then an extra-loud rustling, followed by a *thump* against the tree trunk right next to her, *really* made her jump out of her skin. Caitlyn peered through the bushes. She saw a small furry animal disentangle itself from the weeds and grasses at the base of the tree, then flop clumsily around.

It was a bat. Not one of those tiny pipistrelle bats that was usually seen flitting through the British night sky—no, this was a big bat, with a body covered in fuzzy light brown fur, a dark, pointy, fox-like face, and bright beady eyes. Caitlyn remembered seeing nature programmes about such creatures... Fruit bats, also known as flying foxes.

She wondered what it was doing here. From what she remembered, fruit bats usually lived in tropical countries and places like Australia... perhaps this one had escaped from a zoo? As she approached it cautiously, wondering if it was hurt, it flopped clumsily to the tree and began climbing upwards, using its claw hands as hooks. She watched it for a minute, then shrugged and returned to the path to continue on her way.

But she hadn't gone several steps when she heard a familiar loud rustle and *thump* against another tree nearby and, when she turned to look, she couldn't believe her eyes: it was the fruit bat again! Flopping clumsily around the base of another tree. In fact, it was making strange noises—if she didn't know better, she would have almost thought that it sounded like it was grumbling in squeaks and snorts.

Weird.

She started walking again and, a few minutes later, when she heard the rustle and *thump* again, her suspicions were confirmed. The fruit bat was trying to follow her through the forest, although it seemed to be having hard time, constantly crashing into trees as it flew amongst the branches. Caitlyn grinned. Maybe the phrase "blind as a bat" was truer than she thought.

Why would a fruit bat be following her, though? Caitlyn frowned, then sighed and gave a mental shrug. Just another of those strange things that had been happening ever since she came to Tillyhenge.

Putting on a burst of speed, she jogged along the path as it wound its way upwards, and soon left the bat behind. Finally, she burst out of the trees to find herself standing on the ridge at the very top of the hill, close to the stone circle. Panting and trying to catch her breath, Caitlyn walked slowly towards the sarsen boulders. She was just about to step inside the circle when she saw who was standing next to one of the stones.

It was Hans van Driesen.

CHAPTER TWENTY-TWO

"Good morning, Miss Le Fey," he said.

"Er... Good morning," said Caitlyn. She didn't really want to join him but, with the friendly way he had greeted her, it would have been downright rude and unfriendly if she hadn't.

"I didn't realise you're an early morning jogger?" he said, noting her shortness of breath.

"Oh... no, I was just... There was a bat in the forest and I was trying to get away from it," said Caitlyn.

"A bat?" The big man's face went pale. He glanced frantically around. "Where? Where?"

Caitlyn looked at him in surprise. "It's probably still in the forest... Are you scared of bats?" she asked, trying not to laugh.

Van Driesen looked embarrassed, scuffing the

ground with one boot. "Well…"

Caitlyn couldn't believe it. The man was a big game hunter who could take on lions and rhinos but was scared of fuzzy little bats? Still, she knew there were people who were terrified of birds—it was a common phobia, right?—so maybe being scared of bats wasn't that unexpected.

"Are you out for a walk?" he asked, obviously keen to change the subject.

Caitlyn nodded. "I woke up early and couldn't sleep. You?"

"The same," he said. "Besides, I'd been wanting to come back and have a look at the stone circle again."

Again. Caitlyn remembered uneasily that he was the one who had discovered Stan Matthews's body.

"They're so fascinating, aren't they?" he continued, gesturing to the circle of rocks around them. "There are so many myths and legends attached to these circles. For example, I've heard that on the dawn of the summer solstice, if you stand in a position where the tallest rock lines up with the shortest and watch the sun rising over the top of the circle, you will see a doorway open to the Otherworld." He gave a laugh. "I just love these quaint old English legends, don't you? Now, with this circle, the tallest rock would be that one. So if you were trying to line it up…"

He took a couple of steps to the side and leaned over, trying to get a better view. As he did so, something fell out of his front shirt pocket and rolled towards Caitlyn. She bent and picked it up. It was a small plastic cylinder, the kind that pharmacies and drug companies use to dispense pills and capsules. Her gaze sharpened as she saw the words on the label:

H. v Driesen
Cardiodarone - 20mg, daily.
Taken with food.

"Are these for you, Mr van Driesen?" she asked as she handed the cylinder back to him.

"Ah yes, those are my heart pills," he said smoothly, reaching a hand to take them. "I've got a bit of a cardiac issue—my heart rate keeps slowing down—so my doctor prescribed those to keep things *ticking* along."

He laughed heartily at his own pun. He had a deep, infectious belly-laugh and Caitlyn felt obliged to laugh politely along with him. Her mind, though, was racing. She remembered James telling her that atropine was found in medication to treat slow heart rates. Did this mean that van Driesen *did* have easy access to the poison which had killed both Stan Matthews and Rob Wiggins?

She thought of the vision she had seen in the chocolate cauldron... that figure walking next to Stan Matthews—could it have been Hans van Driesen? She wished fervently that she could have heard the voices more clearly...

"Is something the matter, Miss Le Fey?" he asked, coming closer to her.

"Um... no." Caitlyn groped for something to say, backing away slightly. "I... I'm just surprised you'd want to come back here. I mean, since you discovered Stan Matthews's body... You know, bad associations."

Van Driesen came closer still. He indicated the stone to their right and said, lowering his voice, "I found him over there, you know. I had just walked up the crest of the hill and saw him almost immediately."

"Um... it must have been a horrible shock." Caitlyn tried to edge away from him.

"Well, it wasn't a pretty sight," he admitted. "Matthews's body was all contorted and his hands were curled into claws. But I'd seen death many times before. When you bring a big beast down, you must be prepared that they will fight for their life. Sometimes you have to wait a long time... a *long* time while they thrash around in the throes of death..." He said it slowly, almost as if he was savouring the thought.

Caitlyn shivered. He was really giving her the creeps now. She was suddenly very conscious of the fact that the stone circle was incredibly isolated, up here on the lonely ridge at the top of the hill. James Fitzroy's words on the first day came back to her: *"...you might want to be cautious about wandering to secluded places alone..."*

Yes, they were very alone. There was nobody around—nobody to hear her scream.

Caitlyn started backing away again but she was brought up short by something hard pressing against her back. It was one of the boulders in the circle, she realised. She was wedged against it, unable to back away anymore, while in front of her, Hans van Driesen came closer still...

Then something swooped clumsily out of the forest and hurtled towards them, squeaking and flapping.

The South African looked up, his face draining of all colour.

"Aaaaaah!" he screamed, flailing his hands around his head. "Get away! Get away from me!" Turning, he bolted down the hill and disappeared.

Next to Caitlyn, there was a loud *THUMP* and something smacked into the stone beside her, making her flinch backwards. She took a deep breath, trying to calm her pounding heart, then peered cautiously around the large boulder. To her shock, she saw an old man in a black suit lying on the grass, out cold.

"Viktor!" she gasped, running around to kneel beside him.

He opened his eyes slowly and groaned. Caitlyn looked at him in confusion. Where had he come from? She definitely hadn't seen him loitering about when she arrived at the stone circle. Surely he couldn't have been hiding behind this rock the whole time, and both she and van Driesen had missed it?

"Ohh..." he groaned again, reaching up to rub his bald head.

"Viktor... Are you all right?" Caitlyn asked.

He moved his hands and legs gingerly whilst Caitlyn watched anxiously. With the frail body and brittle bones of someone his age, she was sure he had broken something in his fall. But to her surprise, he seemed all right.

"I am fine. I was just a bit stunned," he said testily. "A slight miscalculation in my flight trajectory."

"What are you doing here?"

"I have been following you through the forest," said the old man, giving her a dark look. "Not that you made it easy for me..."

"Following me? But... I didn't see anything except that fruit ba—No! You couldn't have been..." Caitlyn stared at him, her mind not wanting to join the dots.

No. No, it couldn't be! It had been hard enough believing that magic was real and she was a witch... now she had to believe that Viktor was a *shape-shifter*?

"You... you were that bat?"

Victor sat up, still rubbing his head, and gave her an impatient look. "Of course that was me! Who else did you think it was? I told you—I am a vampire. We can take on other forms, most commonly *Chiroptera*. That's the order of bats," he added as he saw Caitlyn's blank look.

"You're a bat. A fuzzy fruit bat." A slightly hysterical laugh escaped Caitlyn's lips. She caught herself, burst out laughing again, clamped her lips shut, trying to hold it in, then lost the fight at last and dissolved into giggles.

Viktor bristled. "Young lady, I realise that young people nowadays are sadly lacking in manners but really, I find your attitude deplorably rude and ungrateful! I have been trailing all over, trying to protect you, and have suffered the most ignominious bump to the head in the process—and now you have the audacity to laugh at me?"

"Sorry, Viktor..." Caitlyn gasped and wiped tears from her eyes. "I'm sorry, I'm not laughing at you. I'm just... it's a bit of a shock..." She took a shuddering breath, trying to stop laughing. "I *am* grateful—honestly. It was awesome what you did, scaring Hans van Driesen off like that. I don't know what he was going to do... maybe nothing... but you really did protect me this time."

"Humph!" said Viktor as he got slowly to his feet and dusted himself off with great dignity.

Caitlyn tried to help him but he bristled again and she backed off. He reminded her a bit of the Widow Mags. What was it with all these old people and their fierce pride and independence?

"Now, I would be obliged if you would inform me of your next destination so I can make my own way there directly, instead of trying to follow your meandering route," Viktor said.

"Oh, don't feel you have to hang around with me," said Caitlyn quickly. "I'm just heading back to the chocolate shop now, anyway, so I'll be perfectly safe."

"Hmm... Very well. If you should need me, I will not be far away."

Turning, he hunched over and the shoulders of his black jacket seemed to fold in on themselves. His body blurred, seemed to shrivel and shrink, then suddenly the tall stoop-shouldered old man was gone and in his place was a large fruit bat, with long leathery wings and a fuzzy brown body. It looked back at Caitlyn, gave a grumpy squeak, then took off, flapping clumsily, and disappeared into the forest.

Caitlyn blinked, not quite believing what she had seen. But unless she was having hallucinations, it seemed that old Viktor had been telling the truth all along: he *was* a vampire. A vampire who could change into a bat.

Right. And the scariest thing of all? The fact that that sentence didn't even freak her out anymore. That she accepted it, like it was perfectly normal.

CHAPTER TWENTY-THREE

Caitlyn began to make her way down the hill, back towards the chocolate shop. Then she paused. Slowly, she turned, climbed back to the crest of the hill and looked down the other side. In the distance, she could see the familiar majestic outline of Huntingdon Manor.

Well, why not? She had been told that she was welcome anytime and she did want to check on the kitten. Nothing else, of course. It wasn't like she was hoping to see James Fitzroy or anything... no, no, of course not. She just wanted to make sure that the kitten was all right.

Quickly, before she could change her mind, Caitlyn began walking down the hill towards the manor house. She passed through the formal landscaped gardens and arrived at the rear of the property, near the stables. She hesitated just inside the arch leading into the stable courtyard. No matter what James had said, now that she was here, she felt a bit uncertain about just marching up to the house and asking to see the kitten.

"Can I help you, miss?" asked a stable boy walking past.

"Oh... um... is Lord Fitzroy around?"

The boy shook his head. "He's out riding."

"Ah, right. I... uh... I came to see the kitten," said Caitlyn, feeling a bit stupid. "I mean... we rescued a kitten, me and Lord Fitzroy, and he took it back—"

"Oh, the kitten!" A wide grin split the stable boy's face. "Yeah, you'll find him in the old coach house." He pointed to a building to one side of the stable yard. "Just go on through."

Caitlyn walked across the courtyard and entered the large stone building. It must have once housed the beautiful old carriages that were used when the Manor was first built, but now it seemed to be mostly used for storage, with several pieces of farm equipment in one corner, and piles of feed and large stacks of straw bales in the other. And just by the large wooden doors, lying on a pile of burlap sacks, was an enormous English mastiff. He looked up as she came in and thumped his tail, his wrinkled face creasing into a wide doggie smile.

"Hi Bran," said Caitlyn in surprise. "What are you doing here? I thought you'd be lying in front of some grand fireplace in the main house."

Crouching down, Caitlyn reached out to pat the dog, then she realised that he wasn't looking at her anymore. His attention was fixed on something a few feet away. She turned to follow his gaze and saw a tiny ball of black fur scampering around, playing with wisps of straw.

It was the kitten. She was surprised to see how different it looked. Instead of the shivering, bedraggled little creature she remembered, this kitten looked the picture of health. It was still very skinny but its black fur was fluffy and shining, and its big yellow eyes were bright with mischief. It saw her and scooted over, instantly trying to climb up into her lap.

"Ouch!" Caitlyn laughed as she felt its tiny claws dig in through her jeans. She reached down and lifted the kitten up, holding it at face level.

"*Meew!*" said the kitten, squirming. "*Meew!*"

Caitlyn laughed again. *Feisty little thing!* She put it back down gently, next to Bran, and the big dog looked down at it with a confused expression. It was almost as if the mastiff couldn't quite work out what this little ball of fur was.

"*Meew!*" The kitten shook itself, then reached out a playful paw and swiped the mastiff on the nose.

The giant dog flinched, looked even more bewildered, and then gave an enormous sneeze. The rush of air sent the little kitten rolling backwards towards the straw bales.

"*Meew!*" cried the kitten. Its fur puffed up in alarm

and its little black tail stood up straight like a bottlebrush.

Turning, it darted up the nearest thing it could find, which happened to be the stack of straw bales. Caitlyn was amazed at how quickly the little kitten could climb. It didn't stop until it reached the top, then it turned and peered cautiously back down. Caitlyn got up and held her hand out reassuringly.

"It's all right," she said gently. "Bran sneezed, that's all. You must have tickled his nose. He's not going to hurt you. Come on, little one—come down..."

She stretched up towards the kitten but found that she couldn't quite reach the top of the stack.

"*Meew!*" cried the kitten, hesitating at the edge of the top bale.

Caitlyn wondered if it was going to jump. She knew that cats were supposed to have nine lives and that they could jump from great heights with no problems. Still, the kitten was just a baby and it was a pretty long way down to the ground. Could she catch it if it decided to launch itself off the straw bale? She wasn't sure.

"Hey! Don't jump," she said quickly, waving her hand in front of it. "Wait there—I'll come and get you."

Carefully, she put her foot on the edge of the bottom bale, testing her weight on it. The stack teetered alarmingly.

"Whoa!" she said, quickly getting off.

Okay, she couldn't climb up. Her weight would

force the entire stack to topple over and the kitten might get crushed under the bales of straw. She would have to find another way. Caitlyn looked around, then her face brightened. There was a ladder propped next to the coach house door. She dragged it over and leaned it carefully on the wall next to the stack of straw bales, then climbed up until she was level with the kitten.

"Come on, sweetie..." Caitlyn reached out to grab the kitten. "I'll carry you down."

"*Meew!*" said the kitten, squirming in her grasp.

"It's all right. I'm not going to hurt you... Stop wriggling! Just let me—"

"What on earth are you doing?"

The sound of the deep male voice almost startled Caitlyn off her perch and she had to clutch wildly to regain her balance. She looked down and, to her chagrin, saw James Fitzroy standing at the bottom of the ladder, looking up at her quizzically. He was dressed in riding clothes, like the first day she'd met him, and her breath caught slightly at how handsome he looked.

Then she felt her cheeks grow hot as she realised that he was standing right beneath her, with a full view of her backside. *Oh help.* She was wearing her old jeans again, with the seat worn and faded, and the fabric sagging slightly. She cringed to think what she must have looked like from below. Her bottom must be the size of Botswana. Why did James always have to catch her in the most embarrassing positions?

Her face red, she mumbled, "I'm... I'm just trying to rescue the kitten. It got stuck up here and couldn't get down."

As if mocking her words, the kitten suddenly took a flying leap from the top of the stack. It landed lightly on the ground, rolled over a few times, then got up, shook itself and trotted back to the mastiff, completely unharmed.

Caitlyn flushed even deeper. *Great.* So the kitten hadn't even needed rescuing. She had humiliated herself for nothing. Slowly, she climbed back down the ladder. James reached out a hand to help her down the last few rungs and she made a great show of dusting herself off, unable to meet his eyes.

"Would you like my housekeeper to come and give you a going-over with the vacuum?" asked James at last.

Caitlyn paused in the middle of dusting her legs for the fourth time and sneaked a peek at him. His grey eyes were full of laughter.

"I got up early and decided to go for a walk, so I just threw on any old clothes I could find," she babbled. "I didn't even really brush my hair properly. I—"

"You look fine," he said gently, his eyes warm and smiling.

Caitlyn blushed and looked away. "Um... the kitten has recovered really well, hasn't he?"

"Yes, that little hairball is turning into quite a

handful," said James with a chuckle. "Half my household staff always seem to be busy chasing him around."

"I'm sorry," said Caitlyn. "I didn't realise how much trouble the kitten would give you."

"No, no, they're enjoying it," said James, laughing and waving a hand. "I think everyone's fallen in love with the little monkey. Although he seems to have taken a shine to *you*," he added, watching as the kitten scampered back to Caitlyn and began climbing up her leg, making her wince as its tiny claws dug into the denim fabric. She bent and detached the little baby cat from her thigh, then held it against her chest. The kitten nuzzled her neck and purred like a little engine.

"You're adorable," said Caitlyn, tickling the kitten under the chin. She sighed. "I'd love to adopt you but I'm not living in my own place. And I don't even know how much longer I'll be staying in Tillyhenge."

"You're not leaving us already?" asked James.

Did she imagine it or was there a look of disappointment in his grey eyes?

"I'm not sure what my plans are yet," she hedged. "I was only supposed to stay for a couple of nights at most. I've still got most of my things stored at the hotel in London. And... I guess I should be deciding what to do with Barbara's estate back in the States." She gave him a wan smile. "Things got a bit side-tracked with the murders..."

James nodded. "I'm hoping that will be resolved

soon."

"Oh? Are the police planning to arrest someone?" She gasped and said urgently, "Not the Widow Mags?"

James smiled at her. "You care a lot for that old woman, don't you?"

Caitlyn shrugged and looked down, feeling slightly embarrassed. "Well, I... She seems a bit lonely in that chocolate shop... I mean, she has her daughter, Bertha, and her granddaughter, Evie, of course, and she's more than capable of looking after herself—" she added quickly.

He laughed. "Yes, the Widow Mags is very determined to look after herself. But I know what you mean. There's something about her, in spite of her sharp tongue and grouchy manner... that makes you want to help the old girl and take care of her."

"Have you known her long?" Caitlyn looked at him curiously.

"No, to be honest, I hardly knew her at all when I was a little boy. Of course, I didn't spend a lot of time here at the Manor. My mother preferred our townhouse in London. And then I was away at boarding school a lot of the year," he explained. "And after that, Oxford, then... I was out of the country for a while."

"Yes, I was chatting to Amy Matthews the other day. She said that you were a foreign correspondent for the BBC...?"

"Yes, I was."

She hoped that he would elaborate but he didn't. There was an awkward pause. Then Caitlyn cleared her throat and said, "So... um... the police *aren't* going to arrest the Widow Mags?"

"She's still a suspect," James said. "But fresh evidence has been uncovered which is leading the investigation in other directions."

"What other directions?"

"Inspector Walsh hasn't shared the details with me, but from what I can gather, the police are now focusing on strangers who arrived in the village around the time of the murders. Including yourself, of course. But don't worry, you're not a suspect," he said with a smile.

S*trangers who arrived in the village around the time of the murders...* That would definitely include Hans van Driesen. Caitlyn hesitated, then said:

"I don't know if this is relevant but I met Hans van Driesen at the stone circle this morning."

"You went back there alone?" asked James.

Caitlyn saw his brows drawing together and, to forestall him giving her another lecture, she said quickly, "I wasn't really alone. Viktor was with me. He's a... a friend. He was protecting me."

James went very still. "I see. I hadn't realised that another visitor had arrived in the village. Did he come with your cousin from the States?"

"Oh no, he's someone I sort of met here in the Cotswolds..." Caitlyn trailed off, suddenly realising how suggestive that sounded. She saw from James's expression that he had caught the wrong meaning.

"I hadn't realised that you had a *friend* locally."

"Oh, no! He's not... I didn't mean—"

"You're under no obligation to explain anything to me," said James stiffly. "It's certainly none of my business who you choose to spend your time with or what friends you make." He cleared his throat. "So you saw van Driesen at the stone circle?"

Caitlyn drew back, stung by his cool tone. "Yes," she said in a voice to match his. "And he dropped something while he was there. I picked it up. It was a cylinder of heart pills."

"Oh? Do you remember the name?"

"Cardio-something... Cardiodine? Or Cardiorone? Something like that. Anyway, I was thinking... it could be a source of atropine, couldn't it?"

James frowned. "Perhaps. I think the atropine cardiac treatments are hospital-based, rather than in pill form, but the police would have to confirm that. Thank you for reporting this information," he said formally. "Now, if you'll excuse me, I must contact Inspector Walsh and pass the information on."

He turned and strode out of the coach house. Caitlyn stared after him. What on earth had got into him? One minute he was all warm laughter and friendly banter, and the next, he was like a cold, distant stranger!

She thought back: it was only after she'd mentioned Victor, she realised. He had misunderstood and thought that she was talking about some guy she had picked up. Could it be that James Fitzroy was... *jealous?*

Caitlyn blushed at her own presumption. No, that would mean that he liked her and, in spite of what Pomona had said, there was no way a man like James Fitzroy could fall for a girl like her...

The kitten nuzzled her neck again, bringing her back to the present. She gave it a final cuddle. "Sorry, sweetie," she said. "You have to stay here. You'll have a good home here at the Manor."

She walked over to Bran and gently deposited the kitten next to him. The little cat climbed over the mastiff's enormous front paws and curled up against his massive chest. Bran looked down, a perplexed expression on his face, then he sniffed the kitten very gently.

"*Meew...*" said the kitten sleepily, snuggling even closer.

Bran hesitated, then carefully lowered his great head down next to the kitten. He sighed gustily, then closed his own eyes. A few minutes later, Caitlyn could hear him snoring, accompanied by the faint purring from the kitten nestled against him. She smiled, feeling her heart melt a little.

Turning, she tiptoed out of the coach house and began making her way back up the hill, towards the chocolate shop

CHAPTER TWENTY-FOUR

"Whew!" Caitlyn sank gratefully into a chair. Every part of her ached. She couldn't remember the last time she had felt so tired. Her feet were sore from all the walking she had done that morning, followed by standing around all day; her arms ached from holding paintbrushes and lifting and carrying. And yet together with the physical exhaustion was a great sense of satisfaction. She glanced over at her cousin. Pomona was sprawled on the chair next to her, but she too had a contented smile on her face.

"We did a lot, huh?" she said.

Caitlyn nodded. "Yeah, I can't believe we did it all! When you said you wanted to repaint the walls today *and* put in that window display, I never thought we'd get it all done."

"Now we just need to get some tables and chairs," said Pomona with satisfaction. She waved a hand towards the other corner of the chocolate shop. "We could put a couple there along that wall… and one next to the window to replace the window seat that we lost. Oh, and maybe we could get a couple of bar stools to put next to the counter…"

There was a sound behind them and Caitlyn turned to see the Widow Mags hobbling out of the kitchen, a steaming mug in each hand.

"Here," she said, handing them each a hot chocolate. "This will give you a lift."

They raised the mugs to their lips and sipped slowly. The rich hot chocolate flowed down Caitlyn's throat and spread like a warm glow through her entire body. Suddenly, her head cleared, her fatigue was gone, and she felt as if she could spring up and run a marathon.

"Wow!" said Caitlyn, looking up at the Widow Mags. "What did you put in this? It tastes… incredible. A bit strange but incredible."

The old woman smiled. "It's a special recipe. Hot chocolate with cinnamon and nutmeg, and a hint of cayenne chilli pepper. And a few other extras."

"Man, this is like the best pick-me-up I've ever had!" said Pomona, her eyes wide as she took another gulp. "I've had hot chocolate with chilli in it before, but it tasted nothing like this—"

"Ah, but you have not tasted chocolate the quality of mine," said the Widow Mags. "I only use the finest cacao beans, specially imported from the forests of Ecuador, and pounded into powder by hand. But the secret of the recipe is not only what I put in it but *how* I put it in."

Pomona's eyes widened. "You mean, with a spell?" she asked, delighted.

"A spell is nothing more than a recipe of sorts," the Widow Mags said. "Certain ingredients, in certain quantities, in a certain manner." She turned and fixed her gaze on Caitlyn. "I could teach you to do it too... if you wanted to learn."

There was an uncomfortable silence.

"I... I don't know," said Caitlyn breathlessly. "I haven't really had a chance to think about it..."

The Widow Mags gave her a fierce look. "Think about it."

Then she turned to Pomona and said, almost grudgingly, "The shop looks very nice."

Pomona flushed with pleasure. Coming from the Widow Mags, that was high praise indeed! "Th-thank you," she stammered.

"I'm going out now. Will you be all right for dinner?" the Widow Mags asked gruffly. "I don't know if there's enough food left over from last night."

"You're going out?" asked Caitlyn.

"I have an appointment with the physiotherapist... to help with my arthritis," said the Widow Mags, looking disconcerted at having to admit a weakness. "She lives in a nearby town. Bertha will be arriving in a few moments to take me."

"Don't worry about dinner—we'll manage," said Caitlyn with a smile. She was touched that the old woman was worrying about them. "We can always head down to the pub and grab something there if we get stuck."

The old woman nodded and returned to the kitchen. Caitlyn turned to her cousin and said, "What do you say? Want to go to the pub? The food's not great but it's not too bad."

"Well, actually…" Pomona looked slightly embarrassed. "I've got a date."

"A date? With whom?"

Pomona smirked. "With David Allan."

Caitlyn looked at her in surprise. She remembered the young salesman showing up again earlier that day. The excuse he had given was another cup of hot chocolate but it wasn't hard to guess the real reason for his visit. Especially when Caitlyn had glanced across the room and seen him leaning against the counter, hanging onto Pomona's every word as she prepared the hot chocolate and fluttered her eyelashes at him in her best flirtatious manner. He had looked absolutely besotted. Still, Caitlyn hadn't thought he would ever work up the courage to make the first move.

"Wow, did he ask you out?" she said.

Pomona rolled her eyes in mock exasperation. "I didn't think he was ever gonna get around to it! I kept giving him, like, all these hints and openings, but the guy is just too damn shy… Anyway, he did finally get around to it."

"So where are you guys going?"

Pomona smiled. "A midnight picnic in the woods. It was David's idea. Isn't it romantic? I would never have thought that he'd be the type... but I guess people can surprise you." She winked at Caitlyn. "You know what? He's a really sweet guy. Maybe you're right. Maybe it's time I stopped dating bad boys and went with, like, someone nice." She ignored Caitlyn's cynical look and gestured to her clothes. "D'you think I look okay?"

Caitlyn thought Pomona looked a lot more than okay. Even at the end of a long day, her cousin still looked like she could star in an MTV music video. She had brought a change of clothes and today was dressed in a pair of black denim shorts which moulded itself to her full hips, whilst her orange halter neck top made her tanned skin seem to glow with health. Her honey blonde hair was styled in beachy waves around her face, framing her pretty features.

"Oh no, you look hideous. Those clothes are just too frumpy," said Caitlyn, screwing up her face in mock horror.

Pomona laughed, then got up from her chair. "Okay, I'm just gonna run up and freshen up in your bathroom, put on some more deodorant and fix my hair. If David arrives, tell him I won't be long!"

As Pomona disappeared upstairs, Caitlyn saw three figures enter the chocolate shop. The first two were Bertha and Evie, and her eyes widened as she recognised the third. It was Amy Matthews. She hadn't seen the gamekeeper's wife since yesterday morning, when she had caught Amy in the stillroom. Facing the pretty young woman now, she felt slightly ashamed of her suspicions. It seemed ludicrous to think that Amy Matthews could be a murderer.

"Hi," Caitlyn said, getting up from her chair.

Amy smiled shyly at her. "Hullo. I saw Bertha and Evie coming over so I tagged along." She lifted a ceramic casserole dish. "I made some braised beef stew. I thought... if you and your cousin didn't fancy going down to the pub..."

"That's really nice of you," said Caitlyn, feeling even more ashamed now. "My cousin's going out on a date but I would love—"

"Pomona's going out on a date?" Evie interrupted eagerly. "With who?"

"Er... with me." There was a diffident cough behind them and they turned to see David Allan standing bashfully in the shop doorway. He looked very nervous and, in one hand, he held a bunch of flowers. "Um... Is Pomona around?"

"I'm here!" said Pomona, appearing suddenly through the doorway behind the counter. She sashayed out, followed by the Widow Mags.

"H-hi." David blushed and held out the flowers. "Th-these are for you."

Pomona beamed at him. "For me? How gorgeous! You're such a gentleman, David." She gave everybody a little wave. "Well, don't wait up for us!"

She linked her arm through David's and dragged

him, blushing, out the door. Caitlyn wandered slowly over to the doorway and watched them walk away down the lane. Pomona was chattering away to David while he watched her with a besotted grin on his face. They did look very sweet together. Caitlyn smiled. Who knew? Sometimes the most unlikely romances seemed to spring up out of nowhere. She smiled again as she watched them getting smaller in the distance, Pomona's voice fading now, but she could still hear David laughing, a deep laugh which seemed slightly incongruous from such a shy, weedy guy.

Caitlyn went back into the shop where she found Bertha trying to help the Widow Mags into a coat and the old woman saying pettishly, "Don't fuss! I can manage by myself!"

Next to them, Evie was talking to Amy, chatting excitedly about Pomona's budding romance.

"It's so romantic—just like in a novel!" Evie sighed. "Do you think they'll get married?"

Caitlyn burst out laughing. "I think it's a bit early for that, especially if you know anything about Pomona."

"David seems like a nice young man," said Amy. "I mean, even Stan was happy to talk to him, and normally he would have sent door-to-door salesmen packing."

"Don't tell me David was trying to sell you a retirement home as well?" said Caitlyn with a grin.

Amy laughed. "Well, not a retirement home exactly. I came home one evening a few days ago to find him having coffee with Stan. He was trying to get Stan to invest in a development farther up the railway line. The brochure looked beautiful. Modern two-bedroom cottages with built-in wardrobes and fitted kitchens, and a small garden. And they had all these finance plans to help first-home buyers." She sighed, then said bitterly, "Of course, David didn't realise that any money Stan had would go on the drink first." She shrugged. "Anyway, he said he'd be back the next day with more details, but then... Stan got killed that night and I suppose he felt too embarrassed to bother me again." She glanced at her watch. "Oh, I'd better go." She pointed to the casserole dish in Caitlyn's hands. "Make sure you have that while it's hot."

Caitlyn nodded. There was the most delicious smell coming from the dish and she realised suddenly that she was hungry. But even as she looked at the casserole, she had another uneasy thought. Should she have been eating anything from Amy Matthews? It was ridiculous to think that the gamekeeper's wife could be a murderer and yet... Caitlyn couldn't quite push the image of Amy reaching up for the belladonna extract out of her mind.

She looked back at the other woman. Would the poisoner eat her own food? "Won't you stay and have some with me?" she asked.

"No, I've got to get back. I... um..." Amy blushed slightly. "James—I mean, Lord Fitzroy—is coming over tonight. To... to discuss my cottage and my situation. He said he might be able to help me find some work."

"Oh." Caitlyn felt a little stab somewhere inside her. Of course, James would want to help Stan Matthews's widow—she was a tenant on his estate and he was a good landlord. Still, she noticed that Amy looked very pretty tonight, with the bruise on her face now fading and her delicate English-rose complexion highlighted by her soft blonde hair, which had been let down to frame her face. Caitlyn wondered suddenly if James was really coming to see Amy to help with work or for more personal reasons. Then she hastily pushed the thought away. It was none of her business anyway.

A few minutes later, it was just her and Evie left in the chocolate shop. Caitlyn looked at the casserole again, then carefully placed it on the counter.

"That smells delicious! Amy must be a really good cook," said Evie, inhaling appreciatively. She lifted the lid and looked inside. Chunks of tender beef sat in a rich sauce, next to sliced carrots and potatoes.

"Uh... maybe we should eat something else," said Caitlyn hastily, pushing the lid back down over the casserole dish.

Evie looked at her in astonishment. "Why?"

"Um... I've heard that it's really bad to eat beef at night. It's... it's the latest Hollywood secret, didn't you know? No beef after 4 p.m. It's how all the stars stay so slim and toned. It... er... the beef contains proteins that cause cellulite. There's just been a new study that proved that," Caitlyn lied glibly.

"Really?" Evie's eyes were wide. Caitlyn could see the girl's vanity warring with her desire to taste the dish and was relieved when vanity won. "Okay. I guess we'd better not have it then. Such a shame to waste it though."

"We can heat it up again for lunch tomorrow," Caitlyn said, thinking to herself that she'd make sure to throw the stew out in the meantime, when Evie wasn't looking. It *was* a terrible waste of food but... better safe than sorry.

She shut the front door and went around closing the window shutters and tidying up the shop. Evie followed her, chattering excitedly about Pomona—what Pomona had done, what Pomona had said, how Pomona had slept last night, what Pomona had had for breakfast that morning... It sounded like the teenage girl was developing a serious case of hero-worship for her cousin.

Caitlyn only listened with half an ear. Something was nagging her—something more than a poisoned casserole dish... or James coming to see Amy tonight... She felt like there was something she had missed... Something important... but what? Caitlyn frowned. She had no idea.

"...and Pomona is so fabulous! I mean, she just makes things happen, you know?" Evie babbled on. "Blimey, I wish I could be like her! She's not even a witch but she can do all these amazing things—like make men just fall in love with her! I mean, look at David Allan. It was like she cast a love spell on him, wasn't it? And when he wouldn't ask her out, she made him do it!" Evie giggled. "She told me the secret is to get men thinking you're special and mysterious. Like the way she told David she saw a vision of Stan Matthews with the murderer—"

"What?" Caitlyn froze. "Evie—what did you say?"

Evie blinked at her in surprise. "I was talking about the way Pomona got David to ask her out."

"What do you mean? Didn't he ask her out on his own?"

"Well, he was taking ages and Pomona said she got fed up waiting for him to make a move, so she decided she would make herself sound even more interesting and mysterious. She told him that she had psychic abilities and that she had seen a vision of Stan Matthews walking up the hill to the stone circle—with the murderer next to him."

Caitlyn stared at the other girl, an uneasy feeling creeping over her.

"It worked brilliantly!" Evie giggled. "Pomona said David got really interested and kept asking her if she could see the identity of the murderer from her vision. When she wouldn't tell him, he asked her out to dinner."

Caitlyn felt the uneasy feeling turn into a sickening churn in her stomach. Her mind was racing. She closed her eyes and thought of the vision again: *The forest behind the chocolate shop... the outline of the trees silhouetted against the night sky, and the hill stretching up into the distance... and in the foreground... two figures... Stan Matthews... with a dark figure beside him, a hand on Stan's shoulder... the rumble of their conversation... Stan was gesticulating, talking, swearing... the figure throwing its head back and giving a deep belly-laugh...*

Caitlyn gasped and opened her eyes. Now she was seeing another image—this time of Pomona and David walking away down the lane... Pomona chattering away... and David laughing... a deep laugh...

It had struck her at the time. She had thought that it was because it seemed incongruous for such a shy, weedy man to have a laugh like that—but now she realised that that wasn't the reason. It was because the deep laugh had sounded familiar.

It was the same deep laugh she had heard in her vision.

The laugh of the murderer.

CHAPTER TWENTY-FIVE

Caitlyn yanked the front door open and ran down the lane, heading for the village green. But, of course, she knew it was hopeless. They were long gone. She stopped at last and hesitated for a moment, undecided, then she turned and ran back to the chocolate shop. She found Evie still standing in the same place, looking bewildered.

"Listen, Evie—do you know where they've gone?" she demanded. "Did Pomona tell you?"

The other girl shook her head. "N-no... Pomona only said they were going for a night-time picnic, somewhere in the woods. I don't think she knew herself. I think it was meant to be a surprise." She brightened. "But it's a full moon tonight so they're probably going to be in a clearing, where they can get a clear view of the sky."

Caitlyn chewed her lip, trying to ignore the feeling of panic, trying to think. But all she could focus on was how she had missed seeing the truth. It had been right there, under her nose, the whole time. Oh, he had been clever—he had hidden it well. Everyone had only seen a shy, sweet young man. No one had paid him much attention. Not when there were more appealing suspects like the Widow Mags, a witch-like old woman feared by the local villagers, or Hans van Driesen, a swaggering big game hunter who unapologetically admitted that he enjoyed killing animals. Or even Amy Matthews, a poor abused wife who had easy access to belladonna extract and who had great motive and opportunity to kill both victims.

But there had been one other recent new arrival to the village—someone that everyone had overlooked. After all, no one was interested in some boring salesman who was just going around doing his job. They probably didn't even notice or remember him turning up randomly at various houses, knocking on doors, or hovering in the background, because that's what they expected him to do.

And the night he had visited Stan Matthews and had coffee with him, the gamekeeper had ended up dead a few hours later. Caitlyn was willing to bet that David Allan had brought some poisoned chocolates and offered them to Stan. But where had he got the poison?

Then Caitlyn remembered. That day when David

Allan had dropped his suitcase, she had watched Pomona help him pick up the scattered contents. Amongst the stationary and sweets and hand sanitisers was a bottle of eye drops. Yes, *eye drops*. One of the key sources of atropine. And so easy, so innocuous to carry around. So handy for squirting a few drops onto things or... into a cup of hot chocolate.

Caitlyn drew a sharp breath. She remembered something else now. The day Rob Wiggins had been in the chocolate shop, he had been sitting on the window seat next to David Allan. In fact, David had overheard everything the reporter had said to her—in particular, when Wiggins had bragged about knowing the identity of the murderer. The poor guy had probably just been bluffing, but it had sealed his own fate. David couldn't take the chance. So when Angela's drama had caused such a distraction with the chocolate warts, he had taken the opportunity to lean over and squirt a few drops of his deadly eye drop solution into Wiggins's cup of hot chocolate.

And now Pomona was out there, alone, with him.

Caitlyn felt a surge of panic fill her as she realised just why David had asked her cousin out on a date. He believed Pomona's silly story of seeing a vision of Stan Matthews and the murderer. He couldn't risk her revealing his secret—so he was going to silence her, just like he had silenced Rob Wiggins.

"Caitlyn?" Evie was staring at her, starting to look worried now. "Are you okay? Is something the matter?"

"Yes!" Caitlyn took a shuddering breath. "Yes, Pomona's life may be in danger! I think... I think David Allan is the murderer. I don't have time to explain now," she added as she saw Evie's eyes widen and the other girl open her mouth to ask questions. "The important thing is to find Pomona as quickly as possible!"

"My Grandma would know how," said Evie. "She could use magic to find them."

"Can you call her and your mother? Get them to come back?"

"Mum doesn't have a mobile phone. She won't use one—she doesn't like any sort of technology. And Grandma wouldn't have one either." Evie brightened. "But I could try and ring the physiotherapist's place. I'll have to go back home to look for the number but I could try to reach them there or leave a message for them."

"Go! Quick!" Caitlyn shoved her towards the door. "In the meantime, I'll try to get hold of the police."

"There's no police station in Tillyhenge," said Evie. "The nearest one is in the next town and that's miles away. We don't even have a village constable. Mostly, people just go to Lord Fitzroy if there are any problems."

"Okay, I'll... I'll think of something," said Caitlyn. "Just go, quickly!"

The girl took off and Caitlyn was left alone in the chocolate shop. She paced in a circle, her thoughts fluttering like a trapped bird in a cage. What could she do? How could she find them? They were somewhere in the forest—but the forest was vast and twilight was falling. She couldn't just wander around in the dark looking for them. She needed a way to see in the dark, a way to—

"*Viktor!*" she whispered.

Whirling, Caitlyn ran through the cottage and out the back door. She hurried along the path until she reached the edge of the forest.

"Viktor!" she called. "Viktor, are you there?"

Caitlyn strained her ears. Was that a sleepy squeak somewhere? She peered up through the foliage. Yes! There! She could see a fuzzy brown lump hanging from one of the lower branches. She ran over and reached up gently to grab one of the leathery folded wings.

"Viktor! Viktor, wake up!"

The fruit bat woke with a start, squeaking and flapping its wings clumsily, then it lost its grip on the branch and fell to the ground with a *thump*. Caitlyn stepped back and, the next moment, there was an old man in a black suit sitting up in the leaf litter and rubbing his head, whilst looking at her reproachfully.

"Ouch! Must you wake one up in this abrupt manner? I could have—"

"Viktor! You have to help me!" cried Caitlyn, kneeling down next to him. "My cousin, Pomona— she's out there in the forest with a man called David Allan and she's in danger. You've got to help me find her!" She gripped his shoulder desperately. "Bats can see in the dark, right? You can use that echolocation thing and find them for me, can't you?"

"Well, actually, megabats have lost the ability to use echolocation in the course of their evolution," Viktor started to explain pedantically. Then he puffed his chest out. "But never fear. I still have my vampire eyesight. I shall find your cousin for you!"

He stood up, swaying slightly, and made as if to charge into the forest. Instead, however, he charged straight into the nearest tree trunk. *Thunk!*

Caitlyn groaned as she realised the truth. She remembered the way the fruit bat had crashed into tree after tree as it tried to follow her through the forest.

"You're pretty blind, aren't you?" she asked as the old man finally picked himself up again.

"I am a *little* vision-impaired," said Viktor huffily. "But I'm certainly not blind!"

"*Argh!*" Caitlyn clenched her hands in frustration. This wasn't going to work. She needed another way. Another way to find Pomona. Another way to see where her cousin was.

Another way to see...

Caitlyn gasped. *Of course!* She turned and ran back into the cottage.

"Wait... Where are you going?" asked Viktor, shuffling after her.

Caitlyn hurried into the kitchen and up to the hearth, where the enormous cauldron still sat. The ladle was no longer stirring it, but the deep, dark pool of satiny chocolate was still there, swirling gently.

She stepped up to the cauldron, feeling slightly self-conscious and silly. *Okay, here goes nothing*, she thought. She took a deep breath and leaned over, peering into the gleaming pool of dark chocolate. The surface rippled slightly, but remained opaque. Caitlyn tilted her head this way and that, straining her eyes, struggling to see something, anything, in the swirling chocolate. But no matter what she did, she couldn't make the chocolate transform into that deep pool which reflected visions like a "dark mirror".

"Why isn't it working?" she cried out loud, giving the cauldron a frustrated shake.

"Because you don't really believe."

Caitlyn jerked around. The old vampire had come into the kitchen and was standing watching her, an expression of great sadness on his face.

She frowned at him. "What do you mean?"

Viktor made a curious gesture with his hands—a movement filled with wisdom and timeless grace—and for the first time, Caitlyn saw him not as a decrepit, comical old man, but as a dignified ancient guardian.

"Magic can't be treated like a disposable tool. You can't ignore it and ridicule it, and then expect to conjure it up to fulfil your needs at a whim. It doesn't work like that. It needs something from you in return too: sincerity and faith." He shook his head at her. "You say you want to see the vision but you don't really believe it can happen. I can feel your scepticism even from here." He looked her straight in the eye. "Until you really believe in magic—and believe that you are a witch—you will never be able to access the power that's latent within you."

Caitlyn stared at him for a long moment. Then she turned back to the cauldron. She took a deep breath and leaned over once more. This time, however, she closed her eyes for a moment, calmed her breathing, and then opened her eyes slowly and looked—*really* looked—not just with her eyes but also with her heart.

She saw the swirls of chocolate spin and melt together, then gradually start to transform, the ripples flattening out until the gleaming chocolate became a deep, dark pool.

And suddenly, she saw Pomona.

Her cousin was sitting on a blanket spread out on a grassy knoll... she was holding a champagne glass and laughing at something her companion was saying... and in the background, glowing in an indigo sky thick with stars, a huge ivory moon was rising...

The chocolate swirled again and then the vision was gone. Caitlyn took a ragged breath as she stepped back from the cauldron. She saw the old vampire looking at her expectantly.

"I saw Pomona." She swallowed. "I think I know where they are..."

CHAPTER TWENTY-SIX

Caitlyn ran down the darkened lane through the village. There was no time to wait for Evie, no time to wait for the Widow Mags and Bertha to come back. She had to try to find Pomona first. But she hesitated to call the police station. Even if she asked to speak to Inspector Walsh—assuming that he was on duty—she would still have to explain the whole thing to him and get past his scepticism.

What was she going to say? That she knew David Allan was the murderer because of a vision she'd seen in a pot of chocolate? They would think that she was nuts. Even if she did manage to eventually convince the police to help her search for Pomona, it would waste precious time.

No, she couldn't go to the police. But there was someone else who was closer—who might be willing to help her...

She arrived panting at Amy's cottage and knocked frantically on the front door.

"Caitlyn?" Amy frowned when she opened the door and saw her standing there. "Is something wrong?"

James's dark head loomed up behind her, his eyes widening in surprise.

"James!" gasped Caitlyn. "Please—I need your help. He's got Pomona! We need to find her!"

"Who? What are you talking about?" he asked, stepping out and catching hold of her shoulders gently.

The solid weight of his hands was reassuring and Caitlyn felt the panic lessen slightly. She took a shuddering breath and said, "David Allan. He's... he's the murderer. And Pomona's with him."

James's lips tightened. "Where?" he barked.

Caitlyn wanted to cry with relief that he hadn't asked her for explanations. "They're somewhere in the woods. I... I think I know where but I need your help getting there. You're more familiar with the forest. I've got my car parked at the village green. Or maybe we can go in your Range Rover?"

"If you want to move swiftly through the forest, the best way is on horseback," said James. "There are no tracks wide enough for cars and the terrain can become very rough. I've come on Arion—he needed exercise so I rode from the Manor—he's tethered by the pub. Come on."

He grabbed her hand and started for the village

green, pulling her with him. Caitlyn had to run to keep up with his long legs. They reached the open space in the centre of the village and she saw a magnificent grey stallion standing by one of the trees. The horse lifted its great head and snorted as it saw them.

"Can you ride?" asked James as he released the horse from its tether.

Caitlyn eyed the big, powerful stallion warily. It looked absolutely enormous—far bigger than any horse she had seen before. "Um… I've been on pony rides a few times."

"You'll have to hold on a lot tighter," said James with a smile, coming close to her.

Caitlyn stared up at him, her heart pounding. He placed his hands around her waist and lifted her easily into the saddle, then swung himself up behind her. His arms came around her as he grasped the reins, then he kicked the horse into action. Caitlyn caught her breath as she felt the powerful muscles of the stallion bunch and move beneath her. This was so totally different to those sleepy pony rides!

The big stallion snorted and tossed his mane, breaking into an effortless trot as James directed him to the edge of the village. Then, as they entered the open ground near the forest, Arion lurched suddenly into a canter. Caitlyn gasped as she felt herself thrown forwards and gripped the saddle pommel frantically.

"Don't worry—I've got you," came James's deep

voice beside her ear.

Caitlyn felt one of his arms encircle her waist and pull her closer to him. The feel of his body against hers was almost as distracting as the horse's movements. It took all of her concentration to focus on staying in the saddle and not think about the man astride behind her.

They had entered the forest now and James reined the horse in. He looked at Caitlyn with a frown. "You said you know where they are?"

Caitlyn nodded, hoping he wouldn't ask her how. She didn't quite know herself. She pointed to their right. "That way."

James seemed about to say something, then changed his mind and picked up the reins again, urging the stallion forwards. Arion broke into a trot, picking his way confidently through the trees. They had to duck several times to avoid low-hanging branches, although Caitlyn wasn't always quick enough to escape the twigs and leaves scraping at her face. The moon had come out now and its silver light filtered down through the canopy, casting deeper shadows among the trees.

Somewhere an owl hooted, followed by the sharp bark of a fox, but otherwise all Caitlyn could hear was the steady *clop-clop-clop* of the horse's hooves and the soft murmuring of the wind through the trees. She wondered how long they had been riding— shouldn't they have reached Pomona by now? What if she was wrong? What if this instinct—this *magical sense* she was trusting—was nothing more than a figment of her imagination?

Then suddenly, ahead of them, the ground sloped upwards and the trees thinned. The darkness around them lifted as the stallion began climbing the incline, arching his neck, blowing through his nostrils.

They came out suddenly into the moonlight and found themselves on an open grassy knoll. Caitlyn immediately saw the two figures on the other side of the slope, one standing, one lying on the ground, next to the remains of a picnic.

"Pomona!" she gasped, jerking in the saddle.

The stallion neighed sharply and wheeled, side-stepping and pinning his ears back.

"Whoa!" James steadied the horse, then brought him to a stop and jumped down.

Caitlyn barely waited for him to lift her out of the saddle. She hit the ground running and rushed across the open space to where her cousin was lying.

"*Pomona!*" she cried, dropping down next to the unconscious girl. She shook her cousin's unresponsive shoulders, then turned angrily to David Allan. "What have you done to her?"

The young man was barely recognisable. His mild brown eyes were dilated, the pupils black and huge in his bloodless face, and Caitlyn drew back from the darkness she saw in there.

She screamed as David Allan lunged suddenly towards her, but before he could reach her, someone slammed into him, tackling him to the ground. It was James, his own face set and grim as he wrestled the other man onto his stomach and pinned David's arms behind his back. He whipped off his tie and used it to bind David Allan's hands behind his back, then he knotted the other man's shoelaces together.

Caitlyn sagged with relief. She looked back down at Pomona and felt an even bigger wave of relief as she saw her cousin start to stir. The girl groaned and her eyelids fluttered.

"Pomona? Can you hear me?" She bent over her cousin.

"Is she all right?" asked James, coming over.

"I don't know... I hope so," said Caitlyn, gently trying to prop Pomona up. Her cousin's head lolled back. "It's like... she can't wake up."

"She's probably been drugged," said James.

Caitlyn gasped. "You mean—she might have been poisoned?"

"Not necessarily," said James quickly. "She doesn't seem to be exhibiting the symptoms of belladonna or atropine poisoning."

"Yes, but he might have given her something else!" said Caitlyn urgently. "We need to ask David—" She looked behind James's back, then froze. "Where is he?"

James jerked around. They both stared at the empty space on the ground where David Allan had been, then at the empty expanse of grass around them.

"Did you tie him up properly?" demanded Caitlyn.

"Of course I did!" said James, running a distracted hand through his hair. "I know how to restrain a man. It's not the first time I've had to do it. There was no way he could have got out of those knots. Besides, even if he had managed to loosen his hands, it would have taken him much longer to untie the knots in his laces—and without doing that, he couldn't have hobbled far in the short time we'd turned our backs. We would have seen him."

He was right. Besides, Caitlyn could see the tangle of silk tie left behind, the knots still in place. They hadn't been untied. It was almost as if the young salesman had literally shrunk and disappeared within his bindings. By witchcraft. By magic.

Caitlyn shivered. It just couldn't be! And yet there seemed to be no other explanation.

Then, as she stood staring, she saw a movement come from beneath the discarded tie. She peered closer, then recoiled slightly as she realised what it was. A lizard. A small brown lizard with big black eyes that stared unblinkingly at her for a long moment. She shivered again. There was something familiar about those black depths...

Then the lizard turned and scuttled away, disappearing into the undergrowth.

Caitlyn glanced at James. He hadn't seen the lizard and she wondered whether to mention it. She wasn't sure *what* she had seen. A random reptile that had happened to be slinking past? Or...?

"We can't worry about David Allan now," said James, turning back to Pomona. "The police can put out a search for him. The important thing is to get your cousin to medical care first." Then, as he saw the worry in her eyes, he gave Caitlyn a reassuring smile. "Relax. I really don't think she's in any real danger. Her colour's good and her breathing is even. She's probably just been given a strong sedative. It would still be good to get her examined, of course, but I'm sure she'll be fine. She'll probably just have a long sleep."

He bent and lifted Pomona gently in his arms, then started walking towards his horse. Caitlyn followed him and watched as he placed Pomona gently onto the grey stallion, then reached out a hand to help her up.

"Are we all going to ride back on Arion? Can he manage all three of us?" she asked anxiously.

James smiled. "Arion is a Percheron." When Caitlyn looked blank, he added, "They were war horses. They were bred for their strength and speed in battle. He can manage the three of us easily."

Caitlyn nodded and allowed herself to be helped up into the saddle. She sat behind James this time, with her arms around his waist, leaving him free to handle the reins and hold on to Pomona, who slumped in front of him. As Arion snorted and wheeled, then began making his way back into the thick of the forest, Caitlyn turned her head and glanced over her shoulder.

A sense of déjà vu hit her. But this time, she smiled slightly as she knew where she had seen this scene before: in her vision, in the dark chocolate... the vision which had saved Pomona's life.

The horse trotted deeper into the forest. And behind them, the empty expanse of grass on the knoll rippled, looking silver in the moonlight, whilst on the horizon beyond, the full moon hung like a glowing white sphere in an indigo sky thick with stars.

CHAPTER TWENTY-SEVEN

Caitlyn opened her bedroom window and gazed out into the gathering twilight. In the distance, a full moon was rising—still milky and transparent—but growing brighter and larger as it rose above the horizon. She breathed deeply, closing her eyes for a moment, then she opened them again and gazed out at the darkening forest below.

It was hard to believe that only this time yesterday, she and James had been riding through those same woods, searching desperately for Pomona, wondering if they would be in time...

Thank goodness they had been. And James had been right: Pomona had been heavily sedated, but other than sleeping for nearly twenty hours and nursing a woozy head when she finally woke up late this afternoon, she had been fine. In fact, she had been ready to discharge herself immediately and head back to work on the chocolate shop makeover, but James had insisted that she be transferred to Huntingdon Manor, so that she could remain under the watchful eye of his housekeeper while she took it easy for a few days.

At least her cousin seemed to have taken the news of David Allan's real identity in her stride. Pomona had paled slightly when Caitlyn told her what had really happened the night before, but she had rallied quickly, her shock turning to anger and indignation.

"What a jerk!" she had fumed. "Using me like that! I wouldn't be surprised if he *was* a lizard! Pretending to be all shy and sweet when he was just a slimy reptile! I hope someone steps on him and squashes him flat!"

Caitlyn had laughed to herself. Maybe it was a good thing that Pomona fell in and out of love so easily, and her heart was rarely touched, despite all her flirting. At least her cousin wouldn't have nightmares about finding out that her date was a murderer.

There was no doubt now that David Allan had been the one who killed Stan Matthews and Rob Wiggins. The police had already begun to suspect him, particularly as they'd noticed his car parked in odd places, at odd times, around the village. A search of his vehicle that morning had produced his briefcase, complete with a bottle of eye drops containing concentrated atropine sulphate solution, and the police had been delighted; it was further evidence that supported his conviction as the murderer.

Inspector Walsh had instigated a manhunt for the young salesman, but so far it seemed as if he had disappeared without a trace. Even contacting his company, Blackmort Enterprises, only produced the vague message that David Allan had taken indefinite leave. The police were sure they would track him down, but somehow Caitlyn didn't share their confidence. She couldn't help remembering that lizard she had seen, slithering away into the undergrowth...

**

An owl hooted suddenly nearby, startling Caitlyn out of her reverie. She blinked, then drew back from the window and pulled it shut. She heard voices downstairs and wondered who it was. Someone who had come to visit the Widow Mags? It was too late for customers—the chocolate shop was closed—so perhaps it was Bertha and Evie stopping by. Caitlyn hadn't had a chance to speak to them properly since last night and she was keen to catch up on their news. She ran lightly down the spiral staircase and burst through the doorway behind the counter in the chocolate shop, nearly smacking into someone standing on the other side.

"Oh!" She backed away, flushing as she realised

that it was James Fitzroy. "Sorry... I thought..."

"No, the fault is mine," he said, smiling. "I shouldn't have stood so close to the doorway."

She stepped through the doorway again, rubbing her palms on her jeans, feeling suddenly shy. She had hardly seen James since their return from the woods last night. He had been closeted with the police while she had spent most of the night in the hospital, by Pomona's bedside. The closeness they'd shared during that ride through the forest felt like a dream now.

James cleared his throat and said, "I've just come from a meeting with Inspector Walsh. The police are puzzled by something they found. It looks like a piece of parchment with some writing on it, although none of us can read it." He glanced at the Widow Mags, who was sitting at her usual spot behind the counter, and gave a self-deprecating laugh. "Someone suggested that I ask you about it, Mags, seeing as you're the 'resident witch' in Tillyhenge—which I know is all nonsense, of course," he added hastily. "But I thought, since I was passing this way, I'd pop in and see if you and Caitlyn had any ideas...?"

James caught her eye and smiled again, and, for a wild moment, Caitlyn wondered if he might have been using the parchment as a pretext to visit the chocolate shop. After all, he didn't really need to "pass this way" to return to Huntingdon Manor and it seemed silly that he would bother to consult the Widow Mags if he didn't really believe in her witch abilities... so was it just an excuse? To see *her*? Caitlyn blushed and hastily banished the thought from her mind, embarrassed at her own presumption. *No, no, of course not. How could I think that James Fitzroy would be interested in me?*

Hoping her thoughts hadn't shown on her face, Caitlyn focused instead on the photograph that James had taken out of his breast pocket. He handed it to the Widow Mags whilst Caitlyn leaned over the old woman's shoulder to look. The photo showed a piece of parchment, cracked and yellow, with several lines written in faded black ink.

Caitlyn squinted, trying to make sense of the thin, spidery handwriting. Then her eyes widened as some of the words sprang into awful clarity:

...eye of one newt...
...claws of nine bats...
...three feathers from a crow's chest...
...velvet from the White Stag's antlers...
...mixed well with ashes from burning cloves...
...held over ritual fire...

The Widow Mags inhaled sharply. "Where did you find this?" she asked.

James looked surprised at her tone. "It was found in David Allan's car. Tucked into a hidden compartment. Do you know what it is?"

The old woman hesitated, then said at last, "It's a spell."

"A spell?" said James sceptically. He made a face. "Don't tell me that Allan chap was into all that witchcraft nonsense as well?" Then he looked at the Widow Mags curiously. "How do you know it's a spell? Can you read it?"

"Never mind that," snapped the Widow Mags. "Just tell the police to destroy it! Do you hear me? It's very important. They must destroy it!"

James looked doubtful. "The police aren't going to destroy evidence in a murder investigation."

"They *must* destroy it," insisted the Widow Mags.

James sighed. "I'll pass the message along to Inspector Walsh but it's not up to me what the police decide to do." He took the photograph and tucked it back into his breast pocket. "Thank you for that. It was very helpful. Right..." He hesitated and looked around, his gaze sliding to Caitlyn once more. "Right. I suppose I'll say goodnight now." He paused, as if hoping someone would contradict him, but when the Widow Mags remained silent, he turned slowly to go. Then he turned suddenly back to Caitlyn. "Will you be coming over to the Manor to visit your cousin tomorrow?"

"Um... yes, I was planning to," she said, her treacherous heart leaping again, wondering if he was hoping to see her.

"Make sure you use the side entrance in the east wing, which leads into the private quarters. Two thirds of the Manor have been opened to the public and the main entrance is used for tourists—I wouldn't want you to be inadvertently charged a fee for a tour of the Manor," he said with a chuckle.

"Oh... er... thanks," said Caitlyn, trying to hide her disappointment.

"If you ever do want a tour, I'd be happy to give you one myself," he added courteously. He smiled, making her heart give an unsteady flop, then he nodded goodbye to the Widow Mags and left the shop.

When he had gone and the door was firmly shut after him, Caitlyn turned back to the Widow Mags. "What was that spell?" she asked.

For a moment, she thought the old woman wasn't going to answer her either. Then the Widow Mags said, her voice low, "It was black magic. A scrying spell."

"Scrying?"

"A way of seeing the future. Of seeing visions and prophecies."

"Isn't that done all the time, like in crystal balls and things?" asked Caitlyn, thinking of her own experience with the cauldron of dark chocolate.

"Yes, but it is normally done using means that do no harm to others. This is different. It uses dark magic. It harnesses the power of other living creatures, particularly those with magical energy, and subjugates them to your will."

"You mean... those things listed—"

"They had to be freshly killed."

Caitlyn shuddered. Then she thought of something. "The spell... it mentioned the White

Stag..."

"Yes." The old woman nodded. "It is perhaps the most important ingredient. Deer antlers have been prized through the ages for their magical properties and, in particular, for their power of prophecy. And the antlers of the White Stag... a messenger from the Otherworld... a creature known to appear at times of great change and new beginnings... now *that* would give this spell the greatest potency."

Caitlyn drew a breath in. "So Stan Matthews's death *was* connected to the White Stag after all! But not in the mundane way that James thought—no, this has nothing to do with run-of-the-mill poachers or bribery by a big game hunter from South Africa. This was someone who wanted the White Stag for a different reason."

"A much more sinister reason," agreed the Widow Mags. "And David Allan must have thought that Stan Matthews could deliver the creature to him."

"But then maybe he found out that Stan Matthews was just bluffing and killed him in anger or revenge. I wouldn't have been surprised if the gamekeeper just *pretended* to know where the White Stag could be found, just so he could take the money," Caitlyn mused. "Anyway, James told me that the White Stag doesn't even exist."

"Oh, Lord Fitzroy believes that, does he?" asked the old woman with the hint of a smile.

"Yes, he said that there are red deer which are born white, which are a sort of 'white stag'—but there isn't really *a* White Stag, as described in myths and legends," Caitlyn explained.

The Widow Mags said nothing, just smiled again. Caitlyn started to ask something else but they were interrupted by a voice coming from the back door. A moment later, Bertha came from the rear of the cottage and stepped through the doorway behind the counter into the main shop area.

"There's a strange old man loitering about outside the back of the cottage," she complained. "Keeps muttering about looking for his lost teeth."

"Oh, Viktor!" said Caitlyn, suddenly remembering that she hadn't seen the old vampire since the night before.

"You know him?" said Bertha.

Caitlyn gave a helpless shrug. "He's... he's sort of a friend." She hurried out to the cottage backyard and looked around for the old vampire. She owed him thanks for helping her—not in the way she had expected, perhaps, but ironically, he *had* helped her to "see" through the dark and find her cousin.

"Hmm... strange, he's not here," said Bertha, who had followed her out. "He was here a minute ago."

"It's all right," said Caitlyn with a smile. "I'm sure I'll see him around." And she realised that she was actually looking forward to it. Somehow, she had grown very fond of the pompous old vampire.

"Does that mean you're staying in Tillyhenge for a while?"

Caitlyn turned and looked at the older woman. "I

hadn't really thought about it, to be honest. Originally, I only planned to stay a couple of nights, until I got the answers to my questions…"

"Your questions?"

"About my past. About who I am."

"You know the answer to that already," said Bertha with a smile. "You're a witch. You come from a long line of witches, skilled at casting spells and using magic—and with a particular affinity for chocolate." She stepped forwards and took Caitlyn's hand in both of hers. "I hope you will stay on in Tillyhenge, my dear. You need to claim your gift and learn to develop your powers. You need to become the witch you were meant to be. My mother would be able to guide you… she is a great teacher."

Caitlyn swallowed. "But there's more than that, isn't there? I mean, what about my mother? My family? I need to know about them too." She squeezed the older woman's hand. "You both recognised my runestone the other day, didn't you? It means something to you. Can't you tell me, please?"

Bertha hesitated for a long time. Then, very slowly, she reached beneath the collar of her kaftan and pulled something out. Caitlyn gasped as she saw a familiar-looking runestone attached to a length of ribbon.

"You've got one too!" she cried. "How? Why?"

"These runestones have been in my family for generations. I was given mine as a little girl and my—

"

"*Bertha!*"

Bertha started guiltily. They turned to see the Widow Mags standing in the back doorway of the cottage, her expression ominous.

"There are things that should stay in the past," she said, her eyes fierce.

"But Mother—"

"NO."

Bertha fell silent. The Widow Mags looked at them for a moment longer, then she turned and went back into the cottage. Bertha moved to follow, but Caitlyn caught her arm.

"Bertha—"

The older woman gave Caitlyn an apologetic look and shook her head. Then she gently disengaged her arm and said in a bright voice: "I've brought over a hot chocolate recipe for my mother to try. It's one I discovered which mixes Irish whiskey and vanilla with pure raw cocoa, sugar, milk, and fresh cream. Sounds absolutely delicious. You must come in and taste it."

Caitlyn sighed with frustration but nodded and said, "I'll be in, in a minute."

The back door swung shut behind Bertha, leaving Caitlyn alone at the edge of the cottage backyard. She was conscious of a sense of irritation and disappointment. She was sure Bertha and the Widow Mags knew something—something about her mother, something about her family. Why wouldn't they tell her?

A rustle nearby interrupted her thoughts. It had come from the direction of the forest. Caitlyn left the garden and walked slowly towards the edge of the trees, peering up into the branches.

"Viktor? Viktor, is that you?"

Another rustle.

Then something pale moved between the trees, deeper in the woods.

Caitlyn frowned. She strained her eyes, trying to see into the darkness. Almost unconsciously, she took a few steps into the forest, then a few steps more. The pale glow kept moving just slightly ahead of her, almost as if was beckoning her on. She quickened her steps, walking faster and faster, feeling like she would be able to see it if she could just get past the next tree, just scoot around the next bend...

Then she came suddenly into a small clearing deep in the forest.

Caitlyn caught her breath, her heart pounding.

The White Stag stood in the centre of the clearing. Long, slender legs, a sleek, graceful body, and a majestic head crowned by a magnificent set of white antlers... it was breath-taking, an otherworldly creature radiating beauty and magic. It looked at her with limpid dark eyes. The moonlight gleamed on its soft white coat, seeming to outline it in silver.

It took a step towards her and Caitlyn reached out a trembling hand. The White Stag lowered its head and touched her fingers with its nose. Caitlyn felt the velvety softness of its muzzle.

"You're real!" she whispered.

The stag raised its head again and looked at her, its eyes wise and dark. Unbidden, the words came back to Caitlyn's mind:

"...It's believed to be a messenger from the Otherworld and they say it appears to those who are about to set off on a new journey. It's supposed to signal a time of change and new beginnings..."

The magnificent creature looked at her a moment longer. Then it turned and slipped back into the shadows of the forest. A moment later, it was gone.

Caitlyn found that she was holding her breath. She let it out slowly. She wondered if she had been dreaming. But no... she had seen it, felt it. The White Stag had been there. And it had brought her a message.

"I'm staying in Tillyhenge," whispered Caitlyn, and was surprised that she had spoken out loud.

But now that she had said it, she smiled. She knew it was the right decision. It was as if a huge weight had been lifted off her shoulders. Yes, she would stay in Tillyhenge. There were still so many questions she needed answers to—questions about her mother, her family, her past—but she was sure that if she persisted, she would find the answers.

Besides, there was that other thing... the "witch"

thing. With everything that had happened in the last few days, Caitlyn could no longer deny the existence of magic. She couldn't deny that she could be a witch—and she wasn't sure if she wanted to. A part of her was excited at the thought of embracing her new identity. Did she want to be a witch? Learn to work magic? Maybe. But she would never know unless she stayed...

She glanced again towards the darkened trees. The White Stag was no longer visible but she didn't need to see it to understand the message it had brought: she was about to start on a new journey.

FINIS

ABOUT THE AUTHOR

USA Today bestselling author H.Y. Hanna writes fun cosy mysteries filled with humour, quirky characters, clever twists—and cats with big personalities! She is known for bringing wonderful settings to life, whether it's the historic city of Oxford, the beautiful English Cotswolds or the sunny beaches of coastal Florida.

After graduating from Oxford University, Hsin-Yi tried her hand at a variety of jobs, including advertising, modelling, teaching English and dog training... before returning to her first love: writing. She worked as a freelance writer for several years and has won awards for her poetry, short stories and journalism.

Hsin-Yi was born in Taiwan and has been a globe-trotter all her life—living in a variety of cultures, from Dubai to Auckland, London to New Jersey—but is now happily settled in Perth, Western Australia, with her husband and a rescue kitty named Muesli. You can learn more about her and her books at: **www.hyhanna.com**

Sign up to her newsletter to be notified of new releases, exclusive giveaways and other book news! Go to: **www.hyhanna.com/newsletter**

ACKNOWLEDGMENTS

As always, I owe a huge debt of thanks to my wonderful beta readers: Connie Leap, Basma Alwesh, Jenn Roseton and Melanie G. Howe, for their thoughtful feedback and for always finding time to fit me into their busy schedules. They always do so much to help me make each book the best it can be.

And of course, to my wonderful husband for his unwavering support and encouragement, and his belief in me, even when I doubt myself. He is one man in a million.